AFFECTED ᴅʏ ᴀɴ ᴏᴜᴛꜱɪᴅᴇ ꜰᴏʀᴄᴇ

Abandoning any further attempt at speech, he pulled Gavin back to him, taking over the kiss. Hard, urgent, edging toward rough as he tried to find an outlet for that plaguing need for more. He was aware, now, of the rise and fall of his hips, knowing full well what it suggested. He wanted Gavin. God, he wanted him, and just the *wanting* felt intoxicating. He was high, beyond thought or reason, doubt or control.

More, his body demanded, gripping fistfuls of the back of Gavin's shirt, thrusting up against Gavin.

More. Gavin responded, pressing down to meet him.

Derrick leaned back, reclining as far as he could against the sofa, no more concerned with the message he sent by moving toward the horizontal than with the blatant grinding of his hips against Gavin. He drew Gavin down tighter above him, picking up the pace, rubbing against him urgently. The delirious thought occurred to him that he should be thankful he'd jerked off that morning, or this would already be over.

He didn't want it to be over. Not nearly over. He wanted... God, he wanted Gavin's skin. It didn't occur to him to ask first; his hands simply obeyed the imperative without thought or hesitation, releasing their grip on Gavin's shirt at the shoulders to seize it lower, pulling it up.

The way Gavin's body tensed didn't register, not at first, even when Gavin drew back and panted, "Oh, God. Wait... wait."

INERTIA

IMPULSE, BOOK ONE

AMELIA C. GORMLEY

INERTIA

IMPULSE, BOOK ONE

ISBN 978-1479351183
Copyright © 2012 Amelia C. Gormley

Manufactured in the United States of America.

Cover Artist
Kerry Chin (dragonreine.deviantart.com)

Editor
Danielle Poiesz (daniellepoiesz.com)

Cover Layout and Interior Design
Michael Hart (booknibbles.com)

DEDICATIONS

To Paul: *for being loving and supportive and believing I can do it.*
To Tristan: *for understanding the words "Mom's writing."*
To Erin: *for Gavin, and the idea of putting him and Derrick in the modern world.*
To Jenny: *hand-holding, cheerleading, and moral support.*
To Danielle Poiesz, *editor extraordinaire, without whom this would be a far inferior book.*
To Kerry Chin: *for the breathtaking cover art.*

CONTENTS

CHAPTER ONE

A FLASH OF RED HAIR in the sweltering late July sunlight startled Derrick as he pulled into his driveway. A smile spread across his face as the woman sitting on his stoop jumped to her feet and waved energetically.

She pulled open the door of his truck as he turned off the engine, squealing with excitement. Behind the fence between the driveway and the back yard, Chelsea barked.

Grinning, Derrick slid out of the driver's seat and welcomed her with a hug. "What're you doing here, LeeAnn?" he asked when she bounced back a step and gave him room to move away from the car. "Thought we were meeting at the restaurant at six with Devon and Hannah?"

"I got impatient." LeeAnn shrugged, tossing her coppery hair with an irrepressible grin. "Better waiting here for you to get home than sitting back at my mom and dad's place, listening to my mom trot out a hundred different old wives' tales about how to have a healthy pregnancy."

Chuckling, Derrick rounded the back of the truck and pulled his toolkit from the bed. "Well, see, with you being out there on the west coast, she probably thinks all the medical advice you're getting comes from yogis and voodoo witch doctors or something. Figures you need some good old Midwest common sense to balance it all out."

LeeAnn assumed an expression of offended indignity. "I have a perfectly respectable naturopathic OB, I'll have you know." Beneath Chelsea's furious barking at this near-stranger she hadn't seen in years, he almost missed when LeeAnn's eyes twinkled mischievously and she added, "Mom just doesn't need to know I'll be having a perfectly outlandish home birth, as well."

LeeAnn suffered herself to be sniffed by the dog as Derrick opened the gate to the back yard and unlocked the side entrance to the house, dropping his toolkit inside the door before sitting on the sun-warmed concrete step. Shar pei were guard dogs, and though Chelsea was well-trained, Derrick had accepted he'd never quite manage to train her out of barking at least a little when meeting a stranger on her own territory. After a moment, she decided LeeAnn posed no threat and trotted over to greet Derrick.

"So, how is Craig?" he asked as he rubbed Chelsea's massively wrinkled, fawn-sable head.

LeeAnn beamed. "He's fine. Thrilled about the baby. He couldn't make it with me this time, though. He's got a big project that won't be done until August, but I really didn't want to be back in Michigan during the August heat and humidity, and by the time the winter symphony season breaks, I won't be able to travel, so...." She shrugged. "But I wanted to come back and see you before travel and visiting became a lot more complicated by another person."

Derrick smiled as he stood, opening the door again to let Chelsea pass. She headed straight for her food dish, accustomed to their routine despite LeeAnn's presence. LeeAnn followed him, looking around the inside of the red brick house as he fed Chelsea.

"God, this place hasn't changed a bit," she breathed, seating herself at the kitchen table. With the easy manner she'd always had, she made herself at home as if they hadn't seen each other only three times in the last ten years. Despite his customary prickly sense of privacy, Derrick let her. It had been that way since they'd been teenagers. Having her around never felt intrusive as it did with so many others. "I feel like I'm sixteen again, blushing and trying to stammer out an explanation to your grandmother about how we were studying up in your room, when we were actually making out."

Derrick gave a nonchalant shrug. "Yeah, I guess I haven't changed much. Haven't seen the need to."

"You've even kept the appliances. Those were ancient when we were teenagers."

He pursed his lips, nodding. "Most of 'em, yeah. Might remodel the kitchen before long, I guess. Having a hard time finding parts to fix them, they're getting so old."

LeeAnn slanted a glance at him, her huge brown eyes narrowing. "Have you changed anything? Aside from maybe painting?"

"Why should I?" Derrick asked, still giving her a calm look and ignoring a prickle of irritation at having his choices questioned. He opened the avocado-colored refrigerator and handed her a bottle of water. "Not sure I see the point of changing things just for sake of changing them. I'm self-employed, and I have to pay for my own retirement and health and contractor's insurance. If I get injured on the job, I could end up unable to work. The fact that this place isn't mortgaged and that I don't spend money on things I don't need gives me a lot of security."

She looked like she might argue—no doubt something about change being a way to keep things exciting—then stopped herself with a shake of her head. "I swear, Derrick, you're thirty-one going on seventy-five. You have been since we were in the ninth grade."

Any other day, he might have shrugged that remark off, unconcerned for how he appeared to others, but today it felt like an indictment.

Was he boring?

"You've always known that about me, LeeAnn," he murmured, digging in the refrigerator for a bottle of beer and twisting off the top. LeeAnn eyeballed it with a touch of envy, but drank her water dutifully. "You didn't honestly expect that I'd become wild and exciting as I got older?"

11

"I guess not." She sighed, sipping her water. "I always loved that about you, actually. You probably kept me from making a lot of bad choices when we were kids, with all your down-to-earth common sense."

"Then what's the problem?" he asked mildly, lifting his eyebrows.

"I don't know." Her eyes were soft and concerned, and he saw in them the girl he'd once fallen in love with, back when they were fourteen. He'd still been adjusting to the deaths of his parents and the move away from Tennessee and his new life here in Detroit with his grandparents. In those doe-like eyes, he'd discovered someone who would let him be quiet when he needed to be quiet. "I just want to know you're happy, is all."

"'Course I'm happy," he answered reflexively. "I've got a good life here. Got my business, got a dog who's smarter than I am, Devon and I play hockey in the winter together, get together for drinks or dinner once in a while. I'm doing okay."

LeeAnn nodded, apparently accepting his claim even if the agreement didn't completely reach her eyes. She tilted her head inquisitively and reached across the table, lifting a lock of his hair from where it brushed the tops of his shoulders. "This looks really good on you," she said admiringly. "Are you seeing anyone?"

"Nah." Derrick shook his head, brushing the question aside with a shrug, ignoring the put-on-the-spot sensation making his shoulders tense. "Haven't really felt the need."

Her silence spoke volumes, and the squirmy feeling got stronger.

"I'm not good at meeting people, LeeAnn. You know that." He smiled fondly. "You were always my social buffer."

"Well, hell, if that's the issue, while I'm here, we can go out to some gay bars, meet some people. I'll be your wing man."

Derrick groaned. "God, LeeAnn, don't even— No. Just, no. I'm fine alone. I like my life the way it is, okay? I don't need help."

"It's been ten years since we broke up, Derrick. In all that time, have you dated *anyone?*"

He shrugged, scratching at a corner of the label on his beer bottle with his thumb nail.

"Well, what about sex?"

His neck began to heat up. He ignored it. "I've got a good right hand for a reason."

"If memory serves, you've got two *very* good hands. Seems a shame someone's missing out on them," she teased with a saucy grin. Derrick cursed as the blush spread to his face. He hung his head and laughed softly as she chortled in delight at having gotten a reaction from him. "But seriously, honey. I'm kinda worried about you."

"Don't be. I told you, I'm doing okay."

Her mouth tightened as silence fell. She stared, engrossed in her water bottle for a long moment. "Look, you know I didn't break up with you because you were gay, right?"

Derrick blinked. "Wow. That was a quite a non-sequitur even for you."

She waved her hand airily. "Don't change the subject on my change of subject. You do know, right?"

"Bi, if we have to put a label on it, unless you've forgotten that I liked you, too. And yeah, I know."

She didn't lift her eyes. "I always was afraid you thought that, with the timing and everything. I broke up with you not six months after I asked you if you liked men and you told me you did."

"I know," he repeated in that same mellow, modulated tone, taking another drink of his beer. "It never occurred to me you had. Sure, the timing might have seemed odd, but by the time you broke up with me, we'd been having a long distance relationship for three years. Most of those years I barely had time for phone conversations or emails. You were off at college getting worldly and glamorous and I was— Well, I was back here."

"Back here burdened with enough responsibility for four people."

He shrugged. "It was what it was. Over and done."

"I could have chosen my moment better."

"Yeah, it's not like I left you much choice there." Derrick blew out a breath. "Look, did you really come here to hash over the past, LeeAnn? Because, honestly, I'd rather not. Can we just leave that alone, enjoy hanging out while you're here?"

LeeAnn frowned, then nodded. "Right, sorry. That had just been weighing on me for a while now. I could never bring myself to say it before. But yeah. Okay. I got that off my chest, so I'm good. We should get going if we're going to be on time to meet Devon and Hannah."

"Okay." Derrick set his empty beer bottle by the sink to rinse and recycle later. Trying to lighten the mood, he flashed her a grin and dug in his pocket, tossing her the keys to his truck. "Good thing about hanging out with a pregnant woman: designated driver by default."

"I can live with that." LeeAnn laughed, her mood picking up again with the natural resilience her good humor had always possessed. She sobered, though, just for a moment as they stepped back outside, grabbing Derrick's arm as he locked the back door.

"Look, I just—" She pursed her lips, thinking. "I'm going to say this, and then I'm going to let it go. If I worry about you, Derrick, it's because you talk about leaving the past behind, but from where I've been sitting all these years, it looks like you're still living in it. I know with all that happened, your life pretty much stopped when you were eighteen. And I just have to wonder... did it ever start up again?"

She gave him a frank, honest look and lifted herself up on her tiptoes to kiss his cheek, squeezing his arm. Her smile was gentle and encouraging as she turned around and led the way to his truck.

CHAPTER TWO

DID IT EVER START UP AGAIN?

He heard LeeAnn's question again in his mind the next week as he drove out to meet a new client. The last ten years since his grandparents had died and LeeAnn had broken up with him had passed by in an unremarkably comfortable routine. One day dissolved into the next with few, if any, surprises. He liked it that way. He liked the familiarity of it. The rote predictability of it all felt secure.

Which made it strange that he couldn't just dismiss LeeAnn's question out of hand as being one of her fanciful ideas. Back when they were dating, she'd always tried to drag Derrick into new adventures, to draw him out his shell and push him toward novel and exciting things. He'd relied on her for that, as much as she'd relied on his grounded stability to keep her from taking things too far or chasing after something unwise. But that time was long past. He'd grown accustomed to not having the force of her personality behind him, nudging him with gentle concern out of his comfort zone. It never occurred to him to miss it. He'd settled into an uncomplicated life he found agreeable and went about living it day to day.

So why couldn't he ignore her question?

Like much of his business, Mr. Gavin Hayes was a word-of-mouth referral. Unlike Derrick's other clients, however, he wasn't looking for a handyman for repairs. He wanted some carpentry work done, and Derrick had to admit, he liked the idea of doing something different.

Who says I don't shake things up? Building shelves instead of fixing an appliance or plumbing. Everyone look out, we've got a live one, here.

He smiled at his own joke as he rode the elevator up to Mr. Hayes' third-floor renovated industrial loft. A subtle, understated mezuzah hung near the doorbell.

The first things he noticed about Mr. Hayes were his suspenders.

He dressed more like a Manhattan executive on his lunch break than a Detroit businessman. His blue and white striped shirt had an actual white collar and cuffs, with honest-to-God cuff-links rather than buttons. And holding the close-fitting charcoal suit pants up over Mr. Hayes narrow hips were suspenders, rather than a belt.

He looked like something out of a *GQ* spread for the sort of clothes you never found in the local department stores. He looked....

Sexy?

Derrick gave the wayward mental voice a narrow look.

Stylish.

He put on his best attitude of easy-going professionalism, extending his hand.

"Mr. Hayes? I'm Derrick Chance. You called me about some shelves you wanted installed?"

"Of course. Come in."

The second things he noticed were Mr. Hayes' fingers, long, lean and well-manicured. A pianist's hands, LeeAnn would say, putting everything in a musician's context as she was apt to do. If the clothing hadn't been a clue, the handshake would have definitely made it clear that whatever line of work Mr. Hayes was in, it didn't involve manual labor. There was a confidence to the grip of those smooth fingers. They squeezed a little harder at the last instant and lingered in letting go. It made Derrick feel as though he had to grasp for his composure for the second time in half a minute. He didn't *think* he sounded any less calm or professional than usual, but it took a lot more effort to get there.

As he met Mr. Hayes' eyes behind narrow, dark-rimmed glasses, something a little wicked and self-satisfied twinkled in them. Derrick wondered if Mr. Hayes knew he'd thrown Derrick off his stride, and if he was pleased with himself for doing it.

"So, sir, which room did you want the shelves installed in? I'll need to take some measurements, get an idea of the layout."

"Call me Gavin, and the room's this way." Mr. Hayes held out an arm, gesturing down the hall. "Last door on the left before you reach the great room."

"And this is for a home office?" Derrick asked, leading the way. "Tell me about the work you want done."

"Just some basic shelves," Gavin said behind him as they entered the office. It smelled of paint, and small, jagged holes marred the wall. "I'm trying to reclaim the room, make it into something useful." His voice was full of self-deprecating amusement. "But as you can see, I'm really not all that handy."

"That's okay." Derrick shrugged, smiling over his shoulder. Whatever Gavin's talents were, they weren't along the line of home improvement and repair. "That's why you hired me."

"I think I like that decision more all the time," Gavin murmured, a half-grin turning up the corner of his mouth. His gold-brown eyes flicked down Derrick's body before returning to his face.

Derrick went still, trying not to stammer. He'd been out of the dating game for a while, but he was reasonably certain Gavin had just given him the once-over.

"Thanks," he managed after a moment, clearing his throat. He could feel warmth creeping up the back of his neck and prayed it wouldn't reach his face. Grappling for his composure became more difficult when his pulse had picked up and his breath felt a little shorter. Somehow, his casually professional banter had left him feeling like he was on treacherous ground.

He gestured to the damaged wall, scrabbling for safer conversational footing. "You tried to install shelves before?"

"I did." Mr. Hayes laughed, rubbing a hand across his forehead as he sank into the chair by the desk with an eye-catching fluidity. He gestured with an economy of motion that seemed....

Sensual?

Unusual.

"Turns out, I don't know what I'm doing."

Derrick shrugged again, seeking refuge in paying attention to the job at hand before he left Gavin another opening to flirt, if he'd even done so in the first place.

"It's easy enough to repair. We'll make two appointments, one for me to come back and patch the drywall, and another to install the shelves. You still have the primer and paint you used on this wall?"

He unslung his backpack from his shoulder and set it down by his feet, squatting to pull out his tape measure, drafting pad and pencil.

"I do. I can touch it up, that's not a problem."

That was better, Derrick thought as he took the measurements he'd need, noting them neatly on a blank page of his pad. That tingling rush of adrenaline he'd felt when he'd thought Gavin had checked him out faded. Focused on his work, he could regain his equilibrium.

"I was glad to get your call," he said as he juggled the drafting pad, trying to sketch a rough idea of the design he had in mind. "Mostly I handle home and appliance repairs. I don't get calls to do woodwork very often, though I enjoy it. Most people find it easier to buy pre-built shelves, or have them made by cabinetmakers."

Gavin's reply was almost too soft to be heard. "That's a crime."

"Pardon? What is?"

"That you don't get to handle wood as often as you'd like."

"Sorry?" Derrick blinked in confusion, missing the innuendo entirely for a split second before his brain made the connection. Heat raced up his neck and across his face, and that tight, breathless feeling again constricted his chest.

At the instant his face flushed, Gavin's dangerous half-grin made another appearance, white teeth flashing before they caught his bottom lip. He let it slide out from between them, and his eyes gleamed with devilish amusement.

He had beautiful lips.

Shit.

Derrick stared, trying to keep his mouth from gaping open as he struggled to find a calm response that would put them back on professional terms without sounding uptight or censorious.

It could just be a dirty joke. It doesn't mean he's coming on to you.

Right. A dirty joke. That he could handle much better than the idea of Mr. Hayes flirting with him. It might be a little inappropriate for Gavin to be cracking those sorts of jokes to a handyman he'd just met, but some people didn't have many boundaries.

A dirty joke. No problem. Roll with it and keep going. Good-natured professional face on.

Of course, professional face was a great deal more effective when his voice didn't crack on the first syllable.

"He—Here's what I've got in mind for your shelves," he said, holding out the drafting pad. "You wanted them open-ended, right?"

"I did." Gavin accepted the pad, nibbling his bottom lip as he looked over the drawing. As far as Derrick could tell, he was completely at ease. Whatever the reaction sizzling along Derrick's nerves was, to all appearances, it was completely one-sided. "This looks perfect."

He handed the pad back and Derrick added a few notes about the shade of stain to use, taking in the existing woodwork around the room. He squatted again, returning the sketch pad to his backpack and drawing out his day planner.

Gavin smiled. "I haven't seen one of those in years."

Derrick shrugged, flipping to the calendar. "I'm a creature of habit. It'll take me a few days to make the shelves and stain them. Would the end of next week work, to come back and patch the wall and install them? What days would be best for you?"

"Do you do evening or weekend hours?" Gavin asked. "The less time I have to take off work, the better. Friday evening and Saturday would work best for me."

"I make my own hours, so that shouldn't be a problem." Derrick grinned. "If you can get off work a little early on Friday, say late afternoon, I can patch the wall and it'll have time to dry before I come back to install the shelves Saturday."

"I can do that." Gavin nodded, and pulled a phone out of his pocket, beginning to tap the touchscreen. "About four on Friday, then, and three on Saturday?"

Derrick nodded, making notes in his day planner, and slipped it into the backpack. "All right. I'll see you at the end of next week."

He offered his hand, and Gavin unfolded himself from his chair, rising with that unusual grace of his. His grasp was still firm, his palm and fingers still soft, and Derrick's awareness of both seemed to have increased exponentially.

"Next weekend can't get here soon enough," he said smoothly, holding out his arm in invitation for Derrick to precede him back to the door. Derrick blinked, caught flat-footed, unsure how to read or react to the remark.

"I look forward to working with you, too," he murmured, hoping he sounded more professional than he felt. It seemed to take just a little more effort than it ought to, to pull his hand out of

Gavin's grasp. He wasn't sure if it is was his own confused reluctance to let go, or if Gavin really did let the handshake linger.

He felt Gavin's presence behind him like a hot breath on the back of his neck; it became a challenge to resist looking over his shoulder, to see if Gavin was following as closely as it felt he was. He could hear the hissing slide of fabric from Gavin's clothing as he moved.

"I'll call Wednesday or Thursday to confirm," he said, congratulating himself on getting it out without stammering. "Have a good week, Mr. Hayes."

"Gavin." Another flash of that devil-may-care grin accompanied the reminder.

"Right. Gavin." He ducked his head and smiled, unexpectedly abashed. "I'll be in touch, then."

As he walked down the corridor toward the elevator, he wondered if it was just his imagination that made him think it took a long time for Gavin to close the door once he'd left.

CHAPTER THREE

BY FRIDAY, DERRICK MANAGED TO CONVINCE HIMSELF that whatever odd reaction he'd had to his new client, it had been due to factors concocted entirely in his own mind. Only his imagination made everything Gavin said sound flirtatious and laden with innuendo. He didn't know why he'd had the stupid notion that it had been, but he would put a stop to it.

That resolve lasted until the moment Gavin opened the door and shook his hand. Like he'd driven too fast over a short, steep hill, Derrick felt his stomach drop.

It took effort not to stare at the fit of Gavin's navy wool suit pants around his slim hips and thighs as he led the way back down the hall to the office.

"I've actually got a bit of work to do today," Gavin said as Derrick forced himself to pay attention. "But if you'd prefer, I could move my laptop out of here. I wouldn't want to be in your way."

The offer tempted him. If he asked Gavin to leave the room, the confusion and distraction would go away with him. Derrick could do his job and leave. No big deal.

Yet the only thing less appealing than trying to work with that hollow, free-fall feeling in his gut was to try to work without it.

Derrick mustered a casual shrug and a grin he hoped wouldn't give him away. "Unless you've put another hole in the wall over your desk, you won't be in my way."

Gavin blinked, and the cocky smile slid into place. "No, the wall over here's fine. I'll just get to work, then."

He turned back to the open laptop and binders on his desk with one last glance over his shoulder. Derrick turned away, suppressing a confused sigh and digging his joint compound and putty knife out of his toolkit.

The silence as he worked felt awkward and loaded with awareness. He heard the slithering of pages and the tapping of computer keys, but it *felt* like Gavin kept staring at his back. He worked with slow precision, self-conscious and more painstaking than usual, unwilling to make an error in case Gavin was watching. He'd had clients hover over him before with far less impact on his peace of mind or attention to his work.

Finally, he wiped his putty knife clean with a rag he kept in his tool tote and began to put his tools away neatly.

"That's an unusual toolkit," Gavin noted behind him. Derrick froze for a moment, then made himself continue putting things back in their proper places as though unaffected by the fact that Gavin had indeed been watching him.

"Not really. It seems that way because it's not the image most people get when they imagine a toolkit," he answered casually. "Those big steel boxes, they're great and they last forever. Good investment, but it's not a lot of fun hauling them around. No shoulder strap." He grinned, gesturing to the nylon webbing of the strap snaking around the floor by the base of the toolkit.

"So you're a modern-day handyman," Gavin teased. "Giving a hip twist to an old-fashioned profession. Changing with the times."

For an instant, Derrick saw his outdated appliances and furniture back home.

Did it ever start up again?

The memory made Gavin's light-hearted observation seem mocking. He shrugged it off, ducking his head with a self-conscious smile as he collapsed the telescoping trays within the toolkit.

"Not really. I'm actually pretty traditional most of the time. I mean, you saw my day planner, right? This was an impulse buy, about ten years back."

He'd had a few of those, around that time, such as the laser surgery that had corrected his far-sightedness. Coming home from work one day a few weeks after his grandmother's death, the weight of the steel toolkit he'd scavenged out of his grandfather's garage when he'd started his handyman business had seemed too big an inconvenience to be borne. He'd bought the reinforced nylon tool tote that very afternoon.

He rushed past that memory.

"Anyway, I'm finished for today. This'll need to dry overnight." He gestured to the glaring white patches on the gunmetal gray wall. "I'll make sure I sand it first thing tomorrow, get it set for you to prime and paint."

"That sounds good." Gavin unfolded himself from the desk chair, and Derrick wondered again what it was that made the way he moved so unique, or if it was all in his imagination. "You'll be back tomorrow at three?"

Derrick nodded, rising and slinging the strap of his duffel over his shoulder. "Yeah, with the shelves. Looking at the wood you've got in here again, I think I did a good job of matching the stain. I think you'll be pleased."

He braced himself for the lurch in his gut and the tingle that would set in when he accepted Gavin's proffered hand, and discovered for his trouble that there just was no preparing for it.

If Gavin felt it, it didn't show. "That's good news. I can't wait to see it."

"Glad to hear it." He gave Gavin a neutral smile, shaking his hand with what he hoped was a reasonable facsimile of customary easygoing professionalism. "I can show myself out, if you need to get back to work."

"Nah, I'll walk you out, if it's all right with you. I need to go check my mail."

The elevator ride was agony. Gavin leaned against the far wall, looking relaxed and gorgeous with his cuffs rolled up, his freckled forearms lean and lined with veins. Derrick had to force himself not to stare, not to indulge his fascination and try to puzzle out just why he kept reacting to Gavin the way he did. If he could just understand it, maybe he could stop it.

Of course, not staring made it seem like he was avoiding, and that was no good, either. Especially when he felt Gavin's eyes on him, watching him with frank interest. Why couldn't he just make easy, polite small talk, like he did with clients every day? It felt like his tongue was glued to the roof of his mouth.

When the elevator chimed and opened to the ground floor, he suppressed a sigh of relief. He paused to allow Gavin to step out of the elevator first, but Gavin gestured him ahead with a flamboyant wave. "After you."

As he stepped out of the elevator, he heard Gavin murmur, "View is better from back here."

Shit. When he glanced over his shoulder, blushing, Gavin flashed him that mischievous smile. "Red's a good color on you."

Professional. Right. Professional.

"I'll see you tomorrow at three, then," Derrick managed without stumbling over the words too badly. Gavin's grin faltered, for just an instant.

Shit. Had it been rude to ignore the flirtation? Had he offended Gavin?

Before he could apologize, Gavin smiled again. "Looking forward to it." He turned away to his mailbox. Bewildered, Derrick ducked his head and turned away, taking his leave in awkward silence.

Devon hooted triumphantly as Derrick sank the striped eleven-ball in the side pocket, winning the game for Devon on his third turn.

He'd forgotten he was supposed to be solids.

"Wanna play the next one for me, too, bro?" he taunted as Derrick shook his head in resignation, digging a twenty out of his wallet and handing it over.

"What next one?" Derrick snorted, crossing to the barstools along the wall near the pool tables of their favorite bar, refilling his beer glass from the pitcher they shared. He dismissed the notion of another game with a wave of his hand. "That's two out of three to you, man. I'm done."

"Can't be done." Devon lifted one huge, dark-skinned hand toward the flat-screen TV in the corner, where the Tigers duked it out with the Royals. "It's not even the seventh inning yet."

Derrick sipped his beer, watching the TV for a moment. Like half the rest of the state, he, too, was riveted by the Tigers' inching ascent back up to the championship. At the moment, however, nothing exciting was happening. Normally he considered baseball to be precisely his sort of sport. Slow and steady, with occasional moments of rush and activity.

Tonight it just seemed plodding.

"Well, I can't be out late anyway," he said, unable to explain his distraction. "I've got a job tomorrow."

"What?" Devon gave him a disbelieving look. "You never work on the weekends. You said you made it a policy because if you didn't, you'd never have a weekend to yourself. Everyone would want to schedule for Saturday so they wouldn't have to take time off work."

Derrick shrugged. He didn't want to think about how little consideration it had taken to pitch that rule he'd made for himself right out the window. "Had to make an exception this time."

"You can at least hang out until we finish the beer," Devon said.

One corner of Derrick's mouth lifted in a half-smile. "Yeah, I can do that. Just don't ask for another game of pool. I'm liable to forget which ball's the cue."

Devon snorted a soft laugh, the beads on his cornrows bouncing and clicking as he bounded over to his own bar stool. For such a huge man, Devon had the energy of a half-grown Labrador pup. His wife, Hannah, was far more sedate. She joked that she'd hired Derrick to take him out for walks on Friday evenings so she could have a break.

Derrick wondered what drew him toward outgoing people. LeeAnn. Devon.

Gavin.

"Hey." Devon snapped his fingers in front of Derrick's face. "You in there, bro?"

"Yeah, I'm here." Derrick took another slow drink of his beer.

Devon gave him a long, steady look. "LeeAnn made it back to San Francisco okay?"

"Yeah, she posted on Facebook when she got back, said she's beginning rehearsals with the symphony again."

Devon nodded, glancing at the TV as he finished his beer and refilled it from the pitcher. "You've been off in outer space since she visited."

"Yeah." Derrick rolled his glass back and forth between him palms. He stopped when he realized he was making his beer warm. "I've got a lot on my mind."

A non-committal sound was Devon's only reply, and Derrick's lips twitched. They were doing the Guy Thing, he thought with an amused shake of his head. They tip-toed around anything that might be tricky or too emotional, the better to maintain a macho illusion. He'd bet money Devon had probing questions he refused to let himself ask.

Devon had been his best friend since the tenth grade. Derrick had been in the hospital when Devon had broken down sobbing as Hannah lost both ovaries in an emergency surgery for ruptured cysts, ending their hopes for children of their own. Devon was the only friend of Derrick's, other than his neighbor Miss Ingrid, who had been with Derrick at both his grandparents' funerals that bleak winter ten years ago. Not even his older brother had made it home for those.

But when it wasn't crisis time, they skirted around anything too emotional or introspective.

"She thinks my life is at a standstill," Derrick volunteered, letting Devon off the hook. "And I can't manage to convince myself she's wrong."

Devon tipped a shrug. "She could be full of it, too. She's visited, what, three times since college? What does she know about your life?"

"Enough to recognize it hasn't changed in ten years. I'm still where I was before... everything."

"You always talked about doing volunteer work, maybe for the Peace Corps or something, once you didn't have anything else you needed to be here for. What stopped you, back then?"

"I dunno." Derrick stared into his beer glass. "I think I was just too tired, after it was all over. By the time I wasn't so tired anymore, I'd started making a life for myself. I have my business. I have the hockey league in the winter. I help out Miss Ingrid when I can...."

"Well, if it works for you, why change it?"

"I dunno," Derrick repeated, shrugging helplessly. "Maybe it doesn't work for me anymore."

"Then do something else. You've got nothin' holding you back, bro. How hard can it be?"

"Guess you've got a point there." Derrick set his empty glass aside with another wry smile. "Sorry. Compared to what you work with every day this must seem...."

"Like a bunch of White Guy problems?" Devon snorted, waving his hand. "Everyone's got their issues, man. Okay, yeah. I spend my week tryin' to keep street kids fresh out of rehab from goin' back to their pimps or takin' up drugs again. You've seen what I'm up against. You do the repairs and maintenance on our halfway houses without charging for labor—and don't even think I don't know you under-bill for the cost of materials. I'm not gonna accuse you of not havin' any perspective." He shrugged. "Doesn't mean I don't wanna see you happy, bro."

Devon gave him a warm smile and Derrick returned it, then ducked his head, looking down thoughtfully. "Do something else, huh? Just like that?"

"Just like that." Devon lifted his beer in a grinning salute, and drained it.

CHAPTER FOUR

JUST LIKE THAT.

Derrick awoke later than usual Saturday morning, drawn out of a pleasant dream he couldn't remember, one which left his dick hard and aching. It seemed he could still smell the scent he'd caught yesterday when he'd passed close to Gavin as he'd exited the elevator. He gave Chelsea a glower for disturbing him when her breakfast was overdue, wanting nothing more than to sink back down and try to remember and pursue the dream further. Chelsea nudged him again, however, and with a groggy groan, Derrick rose, hitching his straining gray briefs up where they had crept down his hips, and went to fill her dish with kibble.

Usually he was a morning person, waking eagerly, prompt to get started with the day, but today he only wanted to return to bed. Scratching his chest, he shuffled back down the hall, stopping by the bathroom before shutting the bedroom door behind him to guard against another interruption. He crawled back under the covers, hiding from the chill of early morning air that had swept through the house from the windows he left open overnight.

He tucked the pillow under his head and shut his eyes, but it was already too late to get back to sleep, he knew. Instead, he let his mind wander.

It wandered right to Gavin.

Gavin was flirting with him. He was sure of it. That parting shot on the way out of the elevator didn't leave much room for doubt.

And to his surprise, Derrick discovered he liked the idea.

It had been ten years since he'd let himself feel attraction for anyone. He had cut off that part of himself and set it aside. Observations on who might or might not be attractive to him were made on a distant and academic level, acknowledged but never actually *experienced*.

It had been ten years—longer, really—since he'd let himself *react* to anyone, the way he had been doing to Gavin.

It felt good.

He wanted more of it.

He wanted to know if Gavin always smelled the way he had during that brief brush in the elevator. He wanted to see what Gavin's eyes looked like without the glasses.

He wanted to know just what Gavin would say or do next to stop him in his tracks.

The morning wood returned, hard and eager, Derrick reached down and slipped his hand inside his briefs, grasping his cock and stroking once.

God, yes.

He'd become good at this, with more than ten years of celibacy under his belt. It had helped offset the occasional longing for another body, another pair of hands, to try to make masturbating *more*. He tried to make it intimate, rather than just perfunctory. He'd learned to make love to himself.

His hips lifted, moving to meet his grip. He paused only a moment, pushing the covers away and wriggling to shove his underwear down before his hand returned to his dick. He drew it up in a long stroke from root to tip, an accompanying groan sliding from his throat. He cupped his hand over the head and spread the drop of pre-cum collecting at the slit around with slow circles of his open palm before his fingers closed around his cock again. A slight, gentle twist at the top, then gliding down with the foreskin to the base.

His other hand slid across his chest, fingers tweaking and pulling at one nipple, then the other. When the hand on his dick pumped faster, he started to pinch, skirting the edge of actual pain. The touch moved lower, fingertips ghosting along the sensitive skin of his belly and groin.

His knees came up as he spread his legs wider, splaying himself across the bed. He pushed into his own grasp again with a soft grunt, his hips moving in counter-rhythm to his hand, torn between the impulse to draw it out, tease and play with himself, and the need to ease the tension it seemed had been mounting over these past couple weeks. It seemed like forever since he'd fantasized about an actual person. Like feelings of attraction, he'd shut that off. He always stuck to nameless, faceless forms when he imagined another body against his.

This was different. *Better.*

Better to hear Gavin's tenor murmuring flirtatious obscenities in his ear. Better to see those whiskey-brown eyes staring at him as the pleasure built.

A grimace strained his face. The gliding strokes of his hand transformed to hard pumps. He gave himself over to the impulse with abandon.

Jesus. Oh, God… Yeah…

His teeth clenched as he made himself hold back. He didn't want a gentle, mellow orgasm. He wanted it hard and intense. His other hand grabbed his balls, pulling on them from the base, squeezing. He pushed it back, staved it off until the need for release was maddeningly urgent. When it finally forced its way through his restraint, it didn't roll over him, it smashed into him full-force. It ripped itself free from his balls the instant his hand released them and exploded from the head of his cock, splattering his hand, his belly, his chest.

Panting, his muscles quivering, he let his hand fall away from his too-sensitive dick, landing limply on his thigh. The morning air chilled the sweat and semen on his chest as he panted. He opened his eyes, staring up at the ceiling in something a little close to amazement.

And then, feeling wonderfully, gloriously, terrifyingly alive for the first time in as long as he could remember, he began to laugh.

Midway through installing the shelves, he thought he caught Gavin checking out his ass.

He couldn't be completely certain. Gavin may have just turned to glance over his shoulder to see how the installation was going. But Derrick's gut, the feeling of being watched combined with the furtive way Gavin had spun back around to his desk, said otherwise.

Derrick flushed, the instinctive self-consciousness of being the object of someone's attention combining with his own awareness of Gavin. So long since he'd let himself notice anyone, or felt he'd been noticed. What was he supposed to *do* with it?

His awkwardness wasn't helping matters. It was weird to look someone in the eye after masturbating to thoughts of them.

Hey, I barely know you, but I jerked off imagining you this morning. That's not creepy, is it?

It had been so much easier—and far less risky—not to notice, or be noticed.

Gavin worked at his desk again, so Derrick held his silence as he completed the installation with his usual meticulous care. He checked the measurements and level every step of the way to be sure no little inaccuracies crept in. Absorbed in his task, he forgot to be self-conscious, forgot that Gavin might or might not be looking at him.

Which was, of course, the only reason he fumbled and nearly dropped his laser plumb when Gavin spoke.

"Those look really nice. You do great work."

"Thanks." Derrick glanced over his shoulder with a small, pleased smile. Gavin swiveled his desk chair around and watched him with open interest.

"You matched the stain perfectly. How did you do that after just one visit?"

Derrick shrugged, turning back to fitting the final shelf on its support. "I just have a good eye for detail, I guess." He laid his level along the shelf, pleased when the bubble aligned between the marks. He checked the other shelves again, though they had been level as he'd installed them. Then he stepped back, looking at the entire installation with a critical eye.

He was delaying, he realized, frowning at his work. He didn't want to call the job done and leave.

"Something wrong?" Gavin asked.

"Do they look level to you?"

It was a stupid question, and Derrick felt a surge of annoyance with himself for asking it. The level still lay on the bottom shelf where they both could see it, the bubble centered.

Gavin took his time answering. "Yeah, they're level." Derrick nodded, unsatisfied with the response, but unable to find a reason to delay any longer. He grabbed his level off the shelf, squatting beside his toolkit to put it away.

Then Gavin added, "I'm not sure my desk is, though."

Derrick looked up from his bag to the desk on which Gavin's laptop sat. If there was any incline to its surface, it wasn't apparent to the naked eye.

He glanced at Gavin, whose eyes sparkled behind his glasses.

Play along, they coaxed.

Caught somewhere between caution and an amused yearning to join the mischief, he drew his level back out of his bag and laid it on the surface of the desk. As if in on the conspiracy, the bubble hugged the line on the left, resting minutely to the side of center.

Anyone would have called it good enough. It wasn't a significant enough incline to cause any problems working at the desk.

Gavin lifted a challenging eyebrow. "See? Not level."

"No, I guess it's not," Derrick said carefully. It was one thing to be the recipient of Gavin's flirtations, but this was different. This required him to be an abettor, a participant in the game, rather than the passive object of it.

At the least, it was unprofessional. Worse, it meant taking a risk on....

On what?

On whatever might come of it.

How hard can it be? Devon's voice prodded him.

Harder than you think, man.

"I'll just check the leveling feet," Derrick murmured. As flirtatious banter went, he was sure it failed on every single possible level. Gavin watched with quiet amusement and Derrick cursed the blush working its way up from under the collar of his t-shirt as he knelt down by the corner of the desk.

Only once he was on the floor did he consider how it would look, kneeling before Gavin's chair.

If this were a bad porno, I'd be... No. The desk.

He ignored the heat in his face and reached down to the leveling foot, when Gavin murmured, "I think a few of my favorite movies have started out this way."

Derrick swallowed. Shit. Was he that transparent?

His mouth made an executive decision to leave his floundering brain in the dust.

"Think I've seen a few of those," he said softly, all his attention on trying to turn the foot. Anything to avoid meeting Gavin's eyes.

"Is that a fact?" He barely heard Gavin's low reply over the pulse in his ears. Words abandoned him, and he focused on his task instead. He hid behind it until he could figure out just what the hell he thought he was doing here, or why he ever thought he could keep pace with someone who was clearly far better at flirtation than he'd ever be.

"It's rusted," he said, sitting back on his heels and rubbing gritty flakes of iron oxide onto the thigh of his jeans. "That can happen with older desks if the carpet around it's been shampooed."

He dug in his kit for a can of WD-40 and carefully sprayed some around the bolt. It still wouldn't budge. Now what was he supposed to do? He still wanted an excuse to stay, but playing this out any further just might be going overboard. But once he'd begun to play along, it became that much harder to drop the bull.

This is why you don't lie, he scolded himself. *You suck at it.*

"I, um. I could go to the hardware store, get a new foot and replace it, if you wanted. But you'd have to empty out your desk so I could turn it over."

Gavin's expression sobered, as though he detected the shift in Derrick's mood, the sudden uncertainty about carrying this game any further. A small delay to "investigate" the problem was one thing. Making a project of it, taking it to that extreme, was something else entirely.

As he busied himself putting his level away, Derrick added carefully, "That might be a bit more effort than you'd really want to, ahem, put into this."

In his peripheral vision, he saw Gavin shift in his chair, and glanced up to see a troubled look on his face.

Clearly Derrick wasn't the only one questioning the wisdom of carrying this any further.

Despite all his doubts about the strange game they'd started, he couldn't help feel a pang of regret when Gavin murmured, "I don't want to waste any more of your time on a Saturday. It wouldn't be fair."

He bit back a snort. "Only thing I've got planned for the rest of the day is a rousing plate of microwaved leftovers and the Tigers game," he said with a self-effacing chuckle, tucking his drill away in the bottom of the duffel. Only after the words had left his mouth did he wonder if the response made him sound pathetically lacking a life.

He wanted Gavin to give him the go-ahead to do the repair. Just for an excuse to stick around a little while longer, to have a few more of those flirtatious exchanges. But it was ridiculous. The desk was fine. At best fixing it would be a waste of time and money. At worst it could be seen as an unethical means of padding his bill and get him reported to the Better Business Bureau.

The job was done. There was no reason to stay. And judging from the way Gavin took his time responding, Derrick suspected the game had played itself out as far as it could.

It had been fun while it lasted. A break in the usual routine.

"Tell you what," he said, with his usual calm half-smile, trying to find a way to let Gavin off the hook before things got truly uncomfortable. "The desk is usable for now. You have any jobs you need me for in the future, I'll be sure to pick up a leveling foot and bring it with me, replace it free of charge. Call it a bonus for repeat business."

The smile Gavin gave him felt forced. Derrick wondered just what had happened, what had shifted to make what had been a fun game end on such an awkward note. Maybe just the knowledge that they had been close to carrying it too far.

"I can't see why I wouldn't call you again," Gavin answered, recovering smoothly. He pushed himself up from his desk chair in a fluid movement. "You did an excellent job. The shelves are perfect."

"Thank you." He offered his hand to Gavin, slipping on his mask of casual professionalism. The job was over and there was no reason to stay.

You could always ask him out.

The hollow *thunk* in his stomach at the idea wasn't one of the good, exhilarating kind. As new and interesting as it was to dip his toes in the kiddie pool of flirtation, he wasn't ready to dive head-first into the deep end and initiate a date.

Nothing left to do, then, but try to make a dignified exit. Which was made a little harder by his reluctance to release the handshake. It verged on becoming awkwardly long.

"Been a pleasure working with you, Mr. Hayes." He drew his hand back, grasping the strap of his duffel for lack of anything better to do with it. "I've got some paperwork to do, calculating labor time and materials, but I'll send an invoice this week."

"Gavin, and I'll keep an eye out for that."

Derrick ducked his head at the reminder as Gavin gestured for him to lead the way out of the office. "Gavin. Right. Sorry."

"So what is that hint of southern accent I keep hearing in your voice here and there?" Gavin asked as he accompanied Derrick toward the door. That flirtatious note was back.

Derrick smiled. "Tennessee. Lived down there until I was fourteen."

"Just one of those things that never goes away completely, huh?" Gavin's long, elegant fingers wrapped around the door knob. Derrick had to tear his eyes off them, wondering if they were as gentle and deft as they appeared.

He didn't seem in any rush to open the door.

"Pretty much," Derrick said, rubbing the back of his neck under Gavin's inquisitive regard. "My neighbor, Miss Ingrid, is from Sweden. She moved here sixty years ago and you can still hear it in her voice."

"And you've got the southern charm to go with it," Gavin murmured. Before a proper blush could spread up from Derrick's neck, however, Gavin shook his head, something close to regret crossing his face. He turned the knob and held the door open.

"Thanks again. For the shelves."

"Sure. Thanks for your business." Sensing the shift in Gavin's tone, Derrick retreated into his professional persona. "I'll send that invoice along. Take care."

It was over. Whatever that undercurrent of awareness had been, amplified by Gavin's flirty games, it was done. He'd never see Gavin Hayes again. It was time to get back to life as usual.

The idea didn't have the appeal it had once had.

On his way home from his afternoon job on Tuesday, his cell phone rang. He blinked when he saw the caller I.D.

"Derrick Chance."

"Hi. This is Gavin Hayes."

He wasn't sure if he was nervous or thrilled. Maybe somewhere in between. Whatever it was, it took effort to sound professional.

"Sure. What can I do for you? Everything okay with the shelves?"

"Huh? Oh, the shelves are great." The voice on the other end paused, hesitated, and then rushed forward. "I'm having an issue with my dishwasher, though, and I'm hoping you can help me out."

Derrick began to smile.

CHAPTER FIVE

GAVIN WAS AN EVEN LESS PROFICIENT SABOTEUR than he was a handyman, Derrick thought, covering a smile with his hand as he surveyed the damage to the strike plate of Gavin's dishwasher.

And across the kitchen, Gavin leaned on the breakfast bar with his arms folded across his chest and a reckless, challenging grin on his face, waiting to see how he'd react.

Once he felt like he had the urge to laugh under control, Derrick let his tool bag slide off his shoulder and eased down the dishwasher door before squatting next to it.

"Glad I thought to ask the model when you called," he said with an easy-going shrug, pulling out a new strike plate. Business as usual. It had been easy to guess which part was broken from the way Gavin had described the problem. But the deliberate damage caught him off-guard.

So much for not escalating the game.

"See this sort of thing often, do you?" Gavin asked slyly.

He didn't know if he was witty enough to meet Gavin entendre for entendre, but he was damn sure gonna try.

"Nope," he said, pulling out a screwdriver and removing the screws that held the mangled strike plate in place. "Can't say this has ever happened before."

"That's a surprise. I would think your phone would be ringing non-stop for these sorts of repairs." Derrick flushed, but he didn't have long to consider the implied compliment. Gavin's voice was a little softer as he asked, "Should I do something differently to prevent this from happening in the future?"

"Well, what happened here is a sort of fluke." Derrick held up the bent piece of metal, meeting Gavin's eyes as frankly as he could, considering that what they were talking about wasn't actually what they were talking about. "I don't mind the extra work a bit, but I'm sure chances of it happening again are slim. You don't have anything to worry about."

Gavin nodded, biting his lower lip. "Ah. That's a relief."

"Yeah. Maybe next time just try to be a bit more careful with hammers around your dishwasher." Derrick smiled calmly as he looked down, concentrating on screwing the new strike plate in place, before he added, "I brought the leveling feet for your desk, if you still wanted to have that fixed. I've got the time."

He hadn't been certain he would mention that he'd actually brought the parts, not until he saw what Gavin had done to the dishwasher. He'd only bought them because he'd promised he would.

It was worth it, to see Gavin caught off his guard, and the grin that spread over his face as he recovered. "Great. I'll go empty it out, then."

Derrick finished installing the new strike plate and tested it in silence. He wondered just what they thought they were doing. He knew why he had played along; he was intrigued, but the idea of being interested in anyone was just too new, too uncertain, not to let someone more experienced take the lead. But why would a smooth, confident guy like Gavin start all this to begin with? And why did he appear to take a step back every time Derrick rose to the bait?

Maybe he just likes the flirtation for its own sake. Nothing more intended.

Derrick frowned. That seemed the most likely explanation. He had no idea how flirtation and dating worked these days. Not that he'd known all that much last time he'd been involved, either.

Would someone go to the extreme of sabotaging his own appliances just to exchange a bit of banter?

Maybe he's already involved with someone, and the flirtation's just a bunch of "look, but don't touch."

Hell, for that matter, he couldn't even be certain Gavin liked men. He had a certain flamboyance about him, which suggested it was possible, but that could just mean he hovered a little closer to the feminine end of the gender spectrum. He could simply be comfortable enough with his sexuality that he didn't mind flirting with men when he got the chance.

That didn't track either, though. Not in light of the fact that Gavin would pay real money for bogus repairs. Why did he keep trying to talk himself out of the idea that Gavin might be legitimately interested in him?

His frown deepened as he packed up his tools and walked over to the office, leaning against the door frame as Gavin emptied the last drawer of the desk.

"I'm done in the kitchen, if you want to check the repair, see if you find it satisfactory." His words sounded stilted in his own ears, a bit too formal.

Why did he suddenly feel like retreating from all this?

"All right." Gavin stepped away from the desk, making room for Derrick to set down his tool bag and reach down, grasping it to wrestle it to its side. "Do you need any help?"

He shook his head, glancing up. "Nah. Don't want to risk you getting injured."

He blew out a breath as Gavin ducked out of the room. He needed time alone, time to figure out just what the hell it was he thought he was doing. He dug in his bag for a wrench and tightened it around the leveling foot of the desk, trying to find the playful exhilaration he'd arrived with. He didn't realize Gavin had returned from checking out the dishwasher until he over-balanced when the foot snapped off the rusted bolt, sending him falling back onto his ass.

Gavin chuckled behind him. "You're sure you don't need help?"

"Just what is it you think you can do?" Derrick asked with a soft laugh as a blush inched up his neck. He bit his tongue when it occurred to him the answer might sound dismissive, rather than teasing.

Luckily, Gavin didn't seem to be in a mood to take offense. "Oh, I don't know. I'm sure I can contribute something. If only standing here looking pretty."

"Well, we all have our talents," Derrick said under his breath. It was his own moxie this time that caused the tense, nervous fluttering in his gut. Gavin laughed aloud, delighted, though Derrick couldn't be sure if it was due to the underhanded compliment, or the fact that he had begun to give back a little of what Gavin was dishing out.

Silence fell. Gavin watched with undisguised interest while Derrick worked to loosen the rusted bolt. Apparently his instant of daring had been just that: an instant. Now he felt like crawling back inside himself, sure he'd said too much.

"You don't talk a lot, do you?" Gavin asked as Derrick dug his drill and cobalt bits out of the toolkit.

Derrick laughed. "Oh, I dunno, I was just thinking sometimes I talk more than I should. What makes you say that?"

"I don't know. You've got a sort of quiet energy, if that doesn't sound too New Age."

Just how many times a guy could blush in the course of a half-hour before the blood vessels in his face just gave it up as a wasted effort?

"Well, I guess I don't say much, unless I've got something to say. Makes me not a lot of fun at parties. I'm *really* not great with small talk."

Gavin shrugged. "A lot of people feel like they have to fill every silence with noise, no matter how meaningless. I think it's interesting to find someone who isn't afraid of a little quiet."

"Well, speaking of quiet, I'm gonna need to drill this out, which will be anything but. I don't have ear protection for two, so you might want to step out of the room and close the door until I'm done."

Gavin hesitated a moment, then nodded and turned, shutting the door behind him. Derrick frowned, irritated with himself for defeating the purpose of creating an excuse to linger. It seemed pointless to try to draw out the flirtation game and then construct a situation that made talking impossible.

Digging out his safety glasses and ear plugs, Derrick reminded himself again why he didn't lie. Or come up with excuses like these. He wasn't quick enough on his feet to maintain a charade for long. He needed time to think things through, to plan how he would respond.

So why not just ditch the bullshit and ask him out?

Frowning, he began to drill.

Maybe Gavin didn't want to go out. Maybe a little casual banter was as much as he wanted. What did Derrick really know about Gavin, anyway? Maybe it was time to try to get to know him, gauge his interest.

The cobalt bit screeched against the rusted metal of the screw. Derrick worked with silent concentration, unable to make himself *not* do the job with as precisely as he could. Even if it was just a trumped up excuse to spend time with Gavin, he wouldn't be half-assed about it.

Assuming the other feet might be rusted as well, he'd bought enough parts to replace them all. None of the others required drilling out, and he took off his goggles and earplugs after he determined they could be loosened with the wrench. Focused on his task, he forgot why he was there until he heard Gavin behind him.

"Would you like a beer? Or anything else to drink? I could make coffee, or I have juice or water. I don't tend to keep soda around and I only have tea when Andi gets me some."

Startled, he had to catch himself with a hand on the leg of the desk before he fell on his ass again. Gavin was standing in the doorway, holding a foggy brown bottle with the label of the Frankenmuth Brewery. Derrick smiled.

At least he could add *has good taste in beer* to the list of things he knew about Gavin.

"Sure. Just let me finish this first." He gestured to the desk. "If I get injured and my contractor's insurance finds out I'd been drinking on the job, they'd hike my rates sky high, if they didn't just drop me. So. I'll just make sure I'm not actually drinking on the job."

Gavin grinned. "I like the way you think. You didn't have to go to quite so much trouble."

"Well, you know." Derrick shrugged, standing to wrestle the desk upright, then knelt again to adjust the feet, glancing up at the level on the surface of the desk. "Any job worth doing and so on."

"I wish some of the people I work with thought like that." Gavin chuckled, sipping his beer.

"What do you do?"

"I'm an auditor."

"IRS?"

Gavin laughed again. "No. I'm an internal auditor. I'm basically an accountant who double-checks the work of other accountants, mainly to be sure the company *doesn't* end up being visited by our friends at the IRS." He grinned again. "Don't worry. I'm not going to audit you."

"I've got nothing to hide." Derrick grinned and shook his head, glancing once more at the level to be sure he was satisfied before returning his tools to his bag in precise order so he could find them easily next time. Then he wiped his hands on his jeans, brushing off metal shavings. "You're gonna need to vacuum in here. Try not to walk around barefoot until you do. Sorry. If you want, I can do that before I leave, since I made the mess."

Gavin shook his head. "Don't worry about it. Still want that beer? I'll testify you were off the clock, if it comes to that."

"I'd like that," Derrick said, picking up his duffel and following Gavin out to the kitchen, leaning against the breakfast bar as Gavin opened another bottle of beer and offered it to him.

"So, the remodeling you're doing in the office, is that the start of something you'll continue out here?" He gestured around the kitchen and great room with his beer.

A crease appeared between Gavin's brows as he frowned. "No," he said definitely. "What made you think that?"

That tense, twisting feeling slithered its way back into his gut, accompanied by a sickening certainty that he'd put his foot in it. "Oh, well. I don't really know that much about decorating. Just the office doesn't match the rest of the apartment."

The great room was done in monochrome, with the exception of one mismatched and—to Derrick's admittedly inexpert eye—truly hideous painting. Black and white furniture sat on gray carpet before lighter gray walls. The end tables were burnished chrome and glass, and the kitchen appliances and accents were stainless steel. There wasn't a single piece that reflected the antique-looking stain on the desk, which Derrick had so meticulously matched.

"Oh. That. Yeah, I was just trying something different." Gavin's frown eased, and as Derrick watched, he took a drink of his beer and rolled his shoulders once, letting them drop from where they'd begun to creep up defensively. The smile he gave Derrick felt forced. "I doubt I'll extend the theme to the rest of the apartment."

"Okay." Derrick nodded, his tone neutral. He stepped back from that terrified fluttery feeling, behind the impenetrable calm that had become his bulwark these past ten years. He wasn't sure he wanted to risk tracking around whatever he'd stepped in back there with his observation. He didn't know what he'd reminded

Gavin of to cause that reaction, but he was certain he didn't want to find out.

Why had he ever thought this game he'd let himself join in on was a good idea?

"You don't miss much, do you?" he heard Gavin ask, drawing him out of his thoughts before he had the disarray sorted out again.

Derrick shrugged, smiling down at his beer bottle. "I like little details, I guess. That's the thing about being quiet. Lots of time to observe when people think you're gathering wool."

That teasing grin flashed once more. "Now that's almost scary. That would make it hard to keep any secrets from you, wouldn't it?"

Like why this is the second time you've gotten weird and evasive when the office is mentioned?

He couldn't ask that. It was too personal.

Instead, he shrugged again, tilting back his beer. "Not sure why anyone would try. Secrets suck, man. Takes too much energy to keep 'em. I like things simple."

Gavin's eyes glinted with amusement. His small grin broadened into a full-on smile. It took Derrick a moment to catch on, and then the irony of his own words in the present situation struck him.

"Yeah, okay, most of the time," he amended, chuckling as he finished his beer. Anything to keep from noticing just how insanely gorgeous Gavin's lips were.

It was time to leave. Now, before things got awkward and he had to slink away. They were both comfortable and smiling. That was the feeling he wanted to take home with him.

"I should go," he murmured, taking his empty bottle to the sink and rinsing it out. "Thank you for the beer. Same as before, I'll do some calculations on the billing, send you an invoice this week."

"All right." Gavin seemed relaxed and peaceful as Derrick hung the strap of his toolkit over his shoulder. If he was hurt or reluctant for Derrick to go, it didn't show. He gestured down the hall and Derrick led the way. "Thanks. For all the help."

"My pleasure." He shook Gavin's hand, letting himself enjoy the contact, rather than fleeing from it in alarm or confusion. If this was the last time Gavin called him over, he would leave feeling like it was time well spent, something they had both enjoyed, even if they didn't come back for more. Whatever else happened, whether he ever worked up the guts to ask Gavin out or not, at least he'd had this feeling of being in motion again. "Call me anytime."

"I'll do that." Gavin released his hand slowly. Derrick hesitated a second before deciding there was nothing else he could say that wouldn't make things uncomfortable. He gave Gavin a final smile, then he turned and left.

It was a long walk down the corridor before he heard Gavin's apartment door shut.

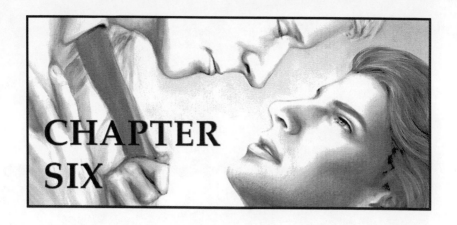

CHAPTER SIX

AFTER A GREAT DEAL OF CONSIDERATION, he only charged Gavin for the replacement part for the dishwasher. He didn't want to appear to be padding his bill with phony labor charges. He also wanted to send the message that he hadn't considered the job "work." He hand-wrote on the invoice *Thanks for your business. I look forward to working with you again.*

As subtle hints went, he was pretty sure it sucked.

He spent the weekend making himself accept that Gavin might not call again, and wondering what he would do if Gavin did.

Ask him out.

Right. It had to be getting to that point, didn't it? They couldn't carry on with the phony repairs much longer, after all.

But why wasn't Gavin asking *him* out? After all, Gavin had been the aggressor in this game they'd been playing.

Tuesday morning, as he loaded lumber in the back of his truck to build a fence for a client, his phone rang. Derrick promptly had cause to be grateful for his steel-toed work boots when the effort to fish it out of his pocket caused him to drop a board on his foot.

It wasn't the sight of Gavin's name on the caller I.D. that made him fumble. Oh no. Of course not.

"Derrick Chance," he said, trying to sound casual as he leaned against the side of his truck and the lumber store manager and clerk took over loading the next stack of boards.

"Derrick, it's Gavin. Uh, Gavin Hayes."

"Yeah, hi, Gavin. How are you?"

"Fine, I'm fine. I just have another problem."

Gavin fell silent, and Derrick heard rustling papers in the background. Was he at work, then? He sounded distracted. Or uncertain. Was he having second thoughts about calling Derrick?

The silence threatened to become uncomfortably long. Finally, laughing to himself at how stupid they were both being about this, Derrick asked, "Well? What's the problem?"

"What? Oh! My toilet. It won't flush. I push down on the thing, and it won't go."

"Mm. Sounds like you've got an issue on your hands there." Holding the phone between his shoulder and jaw, he opened the door of his truck and reached inside for his day planner. He already knew what time he would propose for the appointment, but it gave him something to do with his hands.

"Probably best to get that done today. My afternoon job should be done by four, so I could be there at four-thirty, if you can get out of work a little early?"

"Yeah, I can be there. Thank you. You have no idea how much this means to me."

"Well, broken toilet's nothing to mess with," Derrick teased. He'd bet a month's income Gavin had a second bathroom in that industrial loft of his, and a landlord to handle such repairs. "I'll see you later today."

There was laughter in Gavin's tone as well, when he confirmed the time and hung up. Grinning, Derrick tossed his phone and day planner back on the seat of his trunk and returned to loading the lumber.

Tonight. He'd ask Gavin out tonight.

At four-thirty, sharp, he knocked on Gavin's door. Gavin still wore his suit pants and dress shirt, the sleeves rolled up over his thin, corded forearms. He smiled at Derrick as he opened the door, though, something was missing. Some of his usual cockiness or sass.

"Um, hi. Bathroom's this way," he said, gesturing down the hall. As Derrick preceded him, he heard a chime behind him.

"Tell me what's wrong with it?" he prompted, frowning while Gavin couldn't see him. Why did everything feel different today? There was none of the easy-going fun of their last appointment. He couldn't pinpoint just what was wrong, but the whole thing just felt… off. "It won't flush, you say?"

"Yeah, when I push down on the handle, I hear something rattle around in there, but nothing happens."

"Did you look inside the tank?"

"No, I didn't." Gavin stepped into the bathroom behind him and leaned against the counter. "I just noticed it this morning, and called you after I got to work."

Derrick nodded, glancing over at Gavin. He seemed twitchy. He lifted the porcelain lid to the tank and peered inside, smiling.

A trip-lever didn't just snap like that. Not unless someone had meant to break it.

"It's exactly what I thought the problem was. I brought spare parts, thinking it might be. Lucky for you, it's a quick fix."

"Oh." Gavin didn't sound particularly pleased at that pronouncement. But then that chime sounded again, and with an apologetic look, he fished his smart phone out of his breast pocket, scanning the text message he'd just received. His mouth pulled down in a sharp frown, and Derrick could swear he went a little pale under his freckles.

"Okay," he murmured, still looking at his text messages, his mouth tense and grim. "I'll just leave you to that, then. Excuse me."

Derrick stared after him, a frown tugging at his own mouth. Bewildered as to how to proceed, he worked silently to replace the vandalized trip-lever, then put the lid back on the toilet and picked up his duffel.

He heard the chime of another text message arriving on Gavin's phone as he approached the door to the office. When he peered inside, he noticed a hint of cigarette smoke. Not enough for Gavin to have been smoking in the room, though. Out on the deck, maybe?

Gavin was reading the message, and something raw and wounded tightened his face.

Derrick swallowed and made himself speak. "I'm all done."

"What?" Gavin jumped, startled even though Derrick had spoken softly. He laid his phone onto the desk as though he were pushing it away in self-defense. "Oh. All right. You'll send the invoice again?"

"Yeah." Derrick nodded, studying Gavin. His heart hammered in his chest again, but not with excitement. Not this time.

"Are you...? Is there...? Can I help with anything else?" he asked.

Gavin shook his head. "No, there's nothing—" Mustering a tight, hollow smile, he said with finality. "No. Thank you, though. For coming on such short notice."

"That's not a problem. I'm happy to help. Any time," Derrick said, trying to give the statement a soft emphasis. Trying to let Gavin know that if he was in trouble, Derrick wanted to...

To what?

To do whatever it took to help Gavin smile and laugh and flirt again.

"Thank you," Gavin said with a subdued nod.

Unable to find a reason to stay without prying into things that were clearly none of his business, he left.

"So how's work going, Derrick?"

Stuffed with too many barbecued beef ribs and too much good beer, Derrick leaned back in his lawn chair under the shade of the table umbrella on Devon and Hannah's patio on Wednesday evening. He watched Chelsea romping around the back yard with their border collie, Max. Devon had ducked inside the house to get a round of fresh beers, leaving Derrick alone outside with Hannah.

Derrick felt something inside him stiffen, flinching away and going on full alert at the question. He made himself act as though it hadn't happened, finishing off the warm remnants of his original beer with a forced chuckle. "Oh, you know. Same old. Not much changes when you just fix people's stuff."

"I wouldn't be so sure of that." Hannah filled her glass from the bottle of red wine on the table. While he and Devon had made strides in converting her to a beer drinker, she'd always prefer wine, given her choice. "After all. Most of us work with the same people day-in and day-out. But you encounter new people every day. I'd say your chances of meeting someone interesting are far better than those of us office-bound drudges."

Interesting. Now there's a word for it. Derrick fought not to blush, lifting his bottle to his lips to try to mask the reaction before realizing it was empty. He lowered it again, feeling stupid.

"Oh, come on. I at least get points for use of the word 'drudges,'" Hannah sniffed, giving him a disappointed look, and Derrick realized she'd been trying to make him laugh.

Shit.

Giving himself a mental shake for being bad company, he let his lips quirk into a smile. He pried up the edges of the label on his beer bottle, avoiding her gaze as he tried to think of some way to make an entertaining story out of his encounters with Gavin. Or at least, how to do it without letting on just how confused he was by it all.

Not that he had the first idea what *it* was. Whatever it might be, he wondered if he could discuss it with Hannah without her seeing right through him. Though Devon had been his best friend since high school, it was Hannah who understood Derrick best. Devon and all their other friends were loud, boisterous, and unconstrained when they all hung out together. At their Memorial and Labor Day cookouts, and during the Orphan's Thanksgiving dinner she and Devon hosted each year, Derrick and Hannah would often find themselves encountering each other in a quiet spot away from all the activity, taking a breather. They just got each other.

"Well, I've got a client who's breaking his stuff on purpose."

Hannah lifted her eyebrows. "Oh? Like what?"

One corner pried up, Derrick began to rip off the label in thin strips before he realized the bar code for returning the bottle for the refund was printed on the label. He made himself stop.

"Well, the shelves were the real deal, but there's no way the strike plate on a dishwasher gets round indentations that were made by the head of a hammer by accident. And the trip-lever of a toilet just doesn't snap that way unless someone's putting force on it in ways everyday use doesn't allow for."

"Sounds like a lot of trouble to go to," Devon remarked as he came out the patio door, two frosty bottles of beer in his hands. Derrick accepted his gratefully, hoping it would divert the discussion. But Devon wasn't done yet.

"Maybe he likes you," he added with a shit-eating grin and a waggle of his eyebrows.

Derrick narrowed his eyes at Devon as Hannah spoke, frowning. "Sounds a bit creepy to me. You're sure he's not a stalker or something like that?"

Derrick's eyes widened, and he shook his head quickly. "No. Oh, no. Nothing like that. It's… Well, it's one of those I-know-that-he-knows-that-I-know sorta things. I mean. I've been playing along. Haven't billed him for labor since the first job."

"So he *does* like you," Devon persisted. Derrick closed his eyes, cursing himself for even bringing the subject up.

"I—" He shrugged. He tried to play it off casually and suspected he'd managed to fool no one. He took a long drink of his new beer. "I don't know. Maybe."

"But you're attracted to him?" This from Hannah, looking at him over her wine glass. Out on the grass, Chelsea and Max chased each other and tussled.

He shrugged again, caught somewhere between a defensive instinct to hide inside himself, away from their well-intentioned curiosity, and helpless bewilderment at the sudden turn his life had taken over the past few weeks.

Oh, hey. This beer bottle had a label, too. Fascinating.

"Yeah, guess I am."

"So ask him out." Devon shrugged, chugging his beer carelessly.

Before Derrick could give him a baleful look, Hannah snorted. "It's not always that easy."

"Why not?"

"Well, because Derrick doesn't— He isn't—" She scratched her ear. "Look, honey, not everyone goes through life like a human battering ram like you, okay?"

"What's he got to be afraid of? He's a good-looking guy. Maybe a little rusty on the dating front, but…."

"He *is* a good-looking guy, but sometimes things are a little more complicated…."

Derrick groaned, rubbing his forehead. "While he's flattered about the consensus on his looks, maybe we could not talk about him like he's not sitting right here?"

Hannah slid him an apologetic glance and Devon muttered, "Sorry, bro."

Derrick sighed and shook his head.

"Look. It's not like the idea of asking him out hasn't occurred to me. But, ignoring the fact that I've never asked anyone out in my life, it's—"

"Wait, what? What about LeeAnn?" Devon lowered his beer, lifting his eyebrows. Hannah mirrored the look.

Derrick smiled wryly. "I'm pretty sure LeeAnn just walked up to me one day in the ninth grade and announced I was taking her to the homecoming dance. Next thing I knew, I was in a seven year relationship."

Devon laughed until he wheezed. "That sounds about right," he gasped, trying to catch his breath.

Hannah chuckled and Derrick shook his head, taking another drink of his beer. "Look, it's like Hannah said. Complicated. I have no idea what this guy's story is, except I keep getting the feeling there's something off. I mean, I don't even know if he's single."

"You'll never know unless you ask," Devon said in a patronizing tone that suggested he was convinced he was the only reasonable person on the patio.

"You don't think that'd be, I dunno, unprofessional?"

Devon rolled his eyes. "You're his handyman, not his doctor. Seriously, bro. You're weirding me out here. You're the straightest shooter I know. You don't bullshit, so what's up with all the excuses?"

"I dunno." Derrick shrugged helplessly as Hannah nodded her agreement to Devon's question. Even for friends as close as Devon and Hannah, who were the nearest thing he had to family anymore, it felt too personal to try to explain. He couldn't make himself confess to that rush of pleasure he'd felt when he'd realized Gavin was hitting on him. He didn't want to admit how ten years of resolute solitude now felt foolish and wasted. Choices which had made sense to him when he was twenty-one and exhausted now seemed all wrong.

"It was fun, I guess," he said, knowing it was only a fraction of the truth. "At first. But it's gonna be weird if it goes on any longer, so...." He shrugged again, pushing his hair back behind his ear. "Yeah. Guess I'm asking him out."

Devon grinned proudly, offering Derrick his fist, which Derrick bumped obligingly with his own. That nervous tension was back in his stomach, but being resolved, knowing what he would do, helped. Hannah's eyes seemed understanding as she lifted her wine glass in a silent, encouraging toast.

He spent his morning job Thursday trying to figure out when would be a good time to call Gavin, only to find the matter taken out of his hands when his phone rang as he was on his way to his afternoon job.

"Derrick Chance."

"Hi, it's Gavin Hayes again."

"Hi." Derrick smiled, trying for a tone that was eager, rather than nervous. "Hey, I was just thinking about...."

"Um, I have another job for you. A real job. If you're willing. I can find someone else, if you're not."

Derrick frowned at his phone at Gavin's sober tone. If he'd been hoping for a continuation of their game, it clearly wasn't going to happen.

But maybe there was still an opening here, at least to see what might arise.

"Of course I'm willing. What do you need?"

"There was an accident. With the office door. Now my wall has a hole in it. Would you mind patching it for me?"

"Sure. What time do you get off work?"

"I'm usually home by five-thirty, but I can leave early—"

"No need. I'll be there at six."

"That's not your usual business hours."

"Let me worry about that. See you at six."

The door to the office had been slammed against the wall with such force that the small doorstop in the hinge meant to keep the knob from hitting the drywall had instead been driven into the hollow-core door.

Had Gavin done that?

"That was some accident," Derrick said in as mild a tone as he could manage, closing the door and kneeling to retrieve a flat-head screwdriver out of his toolkit.

"This time it wasn't me, I swear," Gavin said ruefully.

"Okay." Laying the doorstop aside, Derrick replaced the pin in the hinge and looked up at him. "I'll put this in the bottom hinge where the door is sound, for now. There's no way to patch the door. You'll need a new one. If you get one that's got a solid core, this sort of *accident* won't happen again."

"Right." Gavin pushed his glasses up his nose, looking pained. Derrick turned his attention back to the wall, where the handle had punched a large hole in the drywall behind the door. His stomach twisted with an entirely different kind of nervousness, the kind that said something was very, very wrong. Somehow he couldn't quite convince himself that this had happened because someone had bumped the door or fallen against it. The idea that Gavin might have a violent temper was disturbing enough. The other alternative was that there was someone in Gavin's life with a violent temper, and that was even worse.

It had been a long time since he'd felt that protective, nurturing instinct. Living alone, he didn't have much reason to feel it. But now he wanted to comfort and reassure Gavin, to make sure he was safe.

He made himself rein it in; he didn't even know what had happened.

Maybe he assumed too much.

"Someone you live with did this?" he asked cautiously as he began to clear away the loose chunks of drywall still dangling at the edges of the hole by scraps of paper.

Gavin shook his head. "Not anymore. Not for a couple months, actually. My ex. He, um, came over to pick up some of his things he'd left behind. Did that on the way out."

Derrick nodded again, calm and working with a steady hand. That was two questions answered. Now he knew for certain that Gavin was gay, and single. He couldn't seem to bring himself to care as much about those questions, now. He was more concerned with whether or not Gavin was in trouble.

His usual approach to prying into things that weren't his business was simply not to. He couldn't quite manage that, however.

"He's not going to be coming back, I hope?" he murmured, peeling scraps of paper away from the edges of the gypsum.

Gavin smirked, some of the cocky assurance Derrick had first noticed about him creeping back in. "Are you asking if the field is open?"

Derrick smiled, ducking his head to concentrate on his task.

"Actually, I was asking if there was a chance there'd be any more of these accidents in the future," he murmured, for once disregarding the flirtation. Making sure Gavin was safe was more important.

"God, I hope not," Gavin replied with an emphatic shake of his head. "I'm ready to be done with it all, you know? I just want to move on."

Derrick nodded. The words struck a chord of familiarity within him. He grabbed the tub of joint compound out of his toolkit. As always, he felt Gavin's presence at his back, an electric current buzzing along the edges of his awareness as he tried to focus on his task.

"If you have things you need to do, you can go ahead and do it. I won't think you're ignoring me."

"Maybe I just like watching you work," Gavin replied.

"It's not very exciting stuff."

"Doesn't mean I can't admire the view."

Derrick laughed, flushing as he finished patching the hole and began to put away his tools. "Okay, right, so, here I was thinking it was the wrong time, with whatever is going on with your ex and all. I wasn't going to ask, but now you're flirting again, so I'm just gonna go for it." He paused for air and braced himself as he zipped his bag shut, then looked Gavin in the eye. "Would you like to go out with me sometime?"

Gavin blinked and opened his mouth, then closed it again. Derrick gripped the strap to his duffel to keep his hands from shaking with nerves. The longer the Gavin took to answer, the more certain he was he'd screwed up.

"I should have figured you'd just cut through the bullshit. God, I'm an idiot," Gavin murmured almost to himself. That wasn't an answer, though.

Finally Derrick drew a calming breath and shrugged. It cost him to play it off relaxed and casual, but he managed. He thrust his hand out toward Gavin, trying to salvage what little dignity he had left. "Hey. Don't worry about it. Call me in a few days, and I'll come sand this smooth so you can paint, okay?"

Gavin hesitated a moment, then shook his hand. "Look, it's not that—"

"You don't owe me any explanations, Gav," he said sincerely, gripping Gavin's hand a little tighter before releasing it. "It's okay. I'm still happy to help. I'd *like* to help, whatever you need. Seems like you could use a friend. So call me in a few days."

He left before Gavin had a chance to stammer any more awkward attempts at a reply.

CHAPTER SEVEN

WHY HAD HE COME HERE? Derrick wondered, looking around the half-full bar. The bartender made casual conversation with him as he worked, and Derrick answered, though his heart wasn't in it. He made himself talk anyway; the last thing he wanted was to be *that guy* who came to a bar alone and moped. It was time to begin to move his life forward. LeeAnn was right. Ten years ago, worn out and battered by too many losses, he'd just stopped. He'd made a cave for himself, from which he ventured out only to see a few select people, never welcoming anyone else in.

He'd let himself stagnate and called it contentment.

"Is this your first time here?" the bartender asked, rubbing the bar down with a towel. "I haven't seen you around."

Derrick shook his head. "No, but it's been a few years."

"Well, as you can see, we're pretty laid back here."

Derrick chuckled, sipping his whiskey. "Sounds just about my speed."

The bartender smiled. "Well, you know, there's other gay bars around Detroit if people want club music and drag shows. Here, people can just come to hang out and talk. Like the queer answer to *Cheers*. Just a friendly neighborhood pub."

"That's cool," Derrick murmured, listening to the ice clink in his glass. "I'll keep that in mind. I think I'll be trying to get out more, in the future."

"You meeting anyone here tonight?"

"Nope." Derrick shook his head as his cell phone rang, digging in the pocket of his leather jacket. He went still at the sight of the caller I.D. "Excuse me."

He turned away from the bar, thumbing the answer button. "This is Derrick."

"Hi, Derrick. It's Gavin."

"Hi, Gav." He was pleased with his light, casual tone. Pleased that he could roll with Gavin's refusal without sulking or acting like Gavin owed him something. Gavin still needed a friend, that much seemed certain. He'd be damned if he wouldn't at least offer that much. "What can I do for you?"

"I was wondering if your invitation to go out was still open. Maybe we could meet for a drink somewhere. Tonight?"

"Sure, it's still open," he answered, trying to keep his tone mellow even as his pulse sped up. "As long as you don't feel like you have to. I mean it. It's cool if you don't."

He heard a quiet exhalation, not quite a laugh. "I know I don't have to. But, it turns out I really, really want to. Whether I *should* is another subject entirely, but maybe we can talk about that over drinks?"

"Sounds good. You know the Adam's Apple, down on Warren?"

"I've never been there, but I've heard of it."

"Well, I'm already there, if you want to join me. Or we can meet somewhere else."

"No, that sounds fine. I'll be there soon."

Derrick turned back to the bar as he turned off his phone and tucked it back in the inner pocket of his jacket.

"Change of plans?" the bartender asked.

"Yeah." Derrick shook his head, wondering if he looked as bewildered as he felt. "Looks like I'm meeting someone after all."

The bartender pointed to a far corner of the bar. "Tables back there tend to be quieter, when the karaoke begins."

"Thanks. Anyone who joins me, put the drinks on my bar tab." He pushed his glass toward the bartender for a refill, and thanked him with a smile before taking the whiskey back to one of the tables.

If he thought Gavin looked good answering the door of his apartment, it had nothing on the way he walked into a bar. He didn't just dress the part of a man who looked good and knew it. He walked like he owned the place, like he knew every eye was on the narrow-cut black jeans clinging to his hips and the black and red satin brocade vest tailored snugly along the long line of his torso. The effect of all that black contrasted with his pale skin and hair was striking, and Derrick let himself admire for a private moment, as Gavin made his way toward the bar. He only stopped staring when the bartender pointed in the direction of his table in response to Gavin's question.

Derrick stood as Gavin turned to face him, wiping his palms on his thighs.

"Hi." Gavin smiled, and here the facade of confidence developed a flaw, hidden somewhere in the tremulous way his mouth curved and the slight uncertainty in his eyes. "Thanks for letting me join you. For inviting me out in the first place, as well, I suppose."

Derrick smiled, sitting and nursing his whiskey as Gavin ordered one of his own. "I'm glad you decided to take me up on it."

"Yeah, about that." Gavin glanced around the bar, evading Derrick's eyes. "I feel like I should explain."

"I meant what I said. You don't owe me any explanations. If it's not a good time for you to be seeing anyone, say it's not a good time, and that'll be it. I won't be upset. Hell, I'll gladly do the just friends thing, if you'd rather. No expectations." Derrick stared at the ice moving in his whiskey. "Though, I have to say, the flirting might get a bit confusing, there."

Gavin laughed softly. "Now is a bad time for more reasons than I can count, most of which I don't really want to get into at this moment. But—" He paused to thank the waiter and then took a drink of his whiskey, speaking slowly and thoughtfully, "Now is the time you're here, and whether it's a good idea or not, I find myself really interested in you. So. I have a dilemma."

He shrugged, shaking his head with a rueful smile. "I guess I just never expected you to call my bluff."

Derrick chuckled. "Why wouldn't I?"

"Because of that." Gavin gestured to his ruddy face. "You blushed so damn easily. And I gotta give you points for composure, because you played it cool, but I could tell I flustered you. I guess I figured you were too shy, that you wouldn't push it."

"Then why flirt in the first place?" Derrick tilted his head, watching as Gavin squirmed. "I mean, I've been out of the dating scene for a while, so maybe I'm missing something, but I always thought flirting was meant to test the waters."

"I think I had something to prove to myself," Gavin said after a long moment of staring at his drink. "Something my ex said when we broke up kinda took root, I suppose. I wanted to prove him wrong. I didn't count on liking you as much as I ended up doing. I'm sorry."

"So why'd you change your mind?"

Gavin grinned. "My friend, Andi, threatened to kick my ass if I didn't call you."

"Did he, now?"

"She. Andi. Andrea. We were roommates back in college."

Derrick smiled. "Old friends have a way of setting you right when you need it," he murmured, flagging down the waiter for a coffee rather than another whiskey.

"Yeah, they do. She said I needed to get on with my life," Gavin murmured, sipping his whiskey. "So you said you've been out of the dating scene for a while. How long?"

"About ten and a half years," Derrick said, laughing a little at himself.

Gavin stared. "What, you're serious?"

"Mmhm." He thanked the waiter as he brought Derrick's coffee to the table, sipping carefully. It was fresh and scalding hot.

"Were you in a relationship all that time?" Gavin looked bewildered.

Derrick shook his head, pursing his lips. "Nope. I was single." He shifted under Gavin's stare. "It was my choice. The singles scene just didn't seem worth the bother."

"Oh." Gavin seemed a little lost at what to do with this revelation. "That's a really long time. I imagine that's making this a little difficult for you."

Derrick shrugged, smiling. "So far it seems to be going okay."

"Well, I'm glad for that, at least," Gavin said. "So, this bar. Do you come here often?"

"No." Derrick looked around, ignoring the karaoke beginning. "Last time I was here was actually around the time I decided not to bother dating, I guess."

"It sounds like there might be a story to all this."

"There is, though I don't think it's a very uplifting one. Condensed version is, it was Valentine's Day, and I'd had a brutal winter, which had capped off three difficult years. In the middle of it all, my ex had broken up with me, and—" He shrugged, sighing. "I think I just didn't want to be alone on Valentine's Day. So I came here, and people were friendly, but everyone was together and I wasn't really— Well, I mean, I've never been really good with strangers or crowds, anyway, and especially just then at that time in my life, I couldn't—"

"Couldn't what?" Gavin's eyes were gentle, his voice soft. Derrick wondered why he'd told this maudlin story on a date, if that's what this was. He'd never told anyone about that night he had ventured out alone, too lonely to stay home in his newly-empty house and too retiring to bring himself to meet anyone once he was finally out.

Not even Devon knew. He didn't know how Derrick had spent the months that followed his grandparents' deaths and the break-up with LeeAnn, as Derrick found his footing again. After caring for two dying people day and night for three years, he'd had to learn how to live for himself. It had taken a while to figure out who he was when he wasn't taking care of someone else.

He'd never confided any of that in anyone. But it seemed important to revisit that night, when he'd decided he was better off alone. To lay it and everything that had come after to rest.

"Couldn't connect, I guess? Reach out? I don't know. But I wasn't ready, then. I was in a really bad place emotionally and I think maybe I assumed I'd never be able to connect with anyone again, or that it wouldn't be worth the effort if I tried. And by the time I was grounded again, I guess inertia had taken over. Objects at rest and all that. So I never tried. I just wrote the whole thing off. Dating. Relationships. All of it."

"Until now," Gavin murmured.

"Yeah." He sipped his coffee, meeting Gavin's eyes. "And that's not meant to pressure you at all or anything. Just bear with me if it turns out I'm not very good at this."

Gavin flashed him a smile. "You're doing fine so far. I'm glad I called you back."

"I'm glad, too." Derrick ducked his head, sipping his coffee and waiting for his inevitable blush to fade and searching for something a little less weighty to discuss for a while, and to get the subject away from himself. "So. Why'd you become an accountant?"

Gavin grinned, pushing up his glasses with a deliberate flourish. "Because underneath this *smoking fine* exterior, I'm an incredible nerd who likes math."

Derrick spluttered, setting his coffee aside as he laughed, and Gavin feigned affront.

"You'd better be laughing at the classification of myself as a nerd."

"Of course! I wouldn't dare argue the first part. But seriously."

"You don't think I'm serious about enjoying math?" Gavin's grin softened. He gave a lopsided shrug. "I do, actually. Numbers make sense and they challenge me. And yes, I know that is actually quite nerdy."

Derrick's smile softened, studying Gavin closely. Having pride in doing something you liked, something you were good at? Derrick wasn't about to laugh at that. He waved off the idea. "No more nerdy than becoming a writer because you like writing, or a actor because you like acting, or," he gave Gavin a broad grin, shrugging, "becoming a handyman because you like fixing things. I think I'd be more inclined to laugh at someone who chose a job doing something they know they hate."

"Well, now, that raises an interesting question. How did you end up becoming a handyman? I mean, where did you even learn to do all that?"

"From my mom."

Gavin's eyebrows lifted. "Let's hear it for thwarting gender roles. Go on."

"Well, she was the first in her family to go to college. Her uncle had been an old-school repairman who ran his own shop. You know, from back in the day when appliances like TVs and radios and such were too expensive to just throw away and get a new one. She'd helped him in the summers and after school to earn money for college, and then she ended up doing a work-study in the maintenance department of the university. And while she was there, she met my dad and after they graduated and got married, my dad's parents helped them buy this little vacation cabin rental place around Pigeon Forge. Dad did the bookkeeping and mom did the upkeep and maintenance. And I tagged along while she did it."

"That's cool." Gavin smiled. "Are they retired now? What brought you up here from Tennessee?"

Derrick shook his head. "They passed away when I was fourteen. Car accident. I came up here to live with my dad's parents after, because my older brother was in the air force and couldn't be my guardian." He held up a forestalling hand as Gavin's mouth opened reflexively. "Don't apologize or do the awkward, uncomfortable thing. It's okay. It was long ago, and I've dealt with it and you didn't know when you asked."

Gavin closed his mouth, nodding soberly instead. "All right, I won't."

"What about your family? Are they in the area?"

"My mom is. I see her each week. My dad and brother have passed away, and my sister, Meira, is down in North Carolina in college."

"She comes home for holidays?"

Gavin nodded. "Probably not this year, though. She just got an apartment with a roommate and started an internship this summer."

"What's she studying?"

Derrick smiled as Gavin launched into a description of his little sister, toward whom he obviously felt a great deal of affection and pride. From there, the conversation moved on to their hobbies. Gavin discussed the theater companies around the Detroit area he and Andi went to see plays at, and Derrick spoke of coaching the rescued and rehabilitated kids Devon worked with and playing hockey in the winter. Gavin jogged for exercise, and Derrick lifted weights to keep his core toned and avoid a back injury on the job. They bonded over their mutual enjoyment of video games and discussed the pros and cons of console gaming versus playing on a computer. Derrick was on his third cup of coffee when he realized it was already eleven thirty.

"Damn, it's getting late."

Gavin shrugged. "I'm sure the bar is open for at least another couple hours. The karaoke isn't even done yet. So I'll be tired for work tomorrow. I'm in no rush to leave. But if you need to get home...."

Derrick shook his head. "No, I'm not doing anything that would be dangerous if I'm a little groggy in the morning. I just might be a little drowsy when I'm trying to do my billing paperwork in the afternoon. But," he looked down. "I'm having too good a time to go home just yet."

"I am, too," Gavin murmured. Their eyes met, and there was a pulse, an electric feeling that they had said more than the words that came out of their mouths actually meant. Derrick felt as though he'd confessed to just how devoid his life had been of this sort of interaction, and how thrilling and terrifying it was to find it again and discover he enjoyed it so much. He felt exposed, even saying so little.

The silence threatened to become uncomfortable, and the one nagging thought that wouldn't leave Derrick alone seemed too loud to ignore any longer.

"Would I be violating some sort of first date protocol if I asked just how messy this thing was that ended a couple months ago? Am I in danger of stepping in anything?"

Gavin's soft smile faded, leaving him looking a bit stricken. "I won't lie. It's messy. He's not letting go, at least not as quickly as I'd like."

Derrick took his time answering, watching Gavin. He saw the hole punched in Gavin's wall. Was the ex stalking him? Was he violent? Or was Gavin giving off signals that it wasn't as over as he claimed it was? And how did he even try to find that out without getting a knee-jerk denial?

He licked his lips, opting for honesty. "Does he have a reason to think there's something to hold on to, or is he the only one who hasn't go?"

Gavin met his eyes with a haunted gaze. "He's the one not letting go. I refuse to speak to him at all, if I can avoid it."

That didn't sound like a self-deluding denial. Derrick suppressed a sigh of relief as he turned it over in his mind, looking for any clues to the situation he might have missed, and finally nodded. "All right, then."

Gavin opened his mouth and closed it again, then drew a deep breath. "There's more. Stuff you should probably know, but do you think maybe I could save that for another time? I'd kinda just like to enjoy tonight."

Derrick nodded soberly. "Fair enough."

"What about your last relationship?" Gavin asked, nursing his own cup of coffee. "How long were you with that person?"

"From the age of fourteen to the age of twenty-one."

"Oh. Oh." Gavin's eyebrows lifted in surprise, looking a bit troubled. "I can see why you're out of practice then. That must have been quite a blow, wasn't it?"

"Well, it was expected. I wasn't gonna go to college, and she was. Before our senior year, we talked about me going to Boston with her, finding work there, but then Gram and Gramps... needed me and it just wasn't the right time to leave home. So she went and I stayed. After that it was just sort of inevitable that we'd grow apart."

He could think of those three years of slow decline and alienation and increasing distance with philosophical complacency, now. How by the third year, the emails and phone calls had gotten less and less frequent, and he'd stopped feeling he could call her and confide how overwhelmed he felt with the care of his grandparents, until finally they had both acknowledged it was over.

"After that, I looked at the singles scene. Particularly meeting other men, which wasn't something I'd had a chance to explore before. Which is why I ended up here, that time." He gave a self-effacing smile. "But that whole thing, it just isn't me."

"I'm sorry to hear that. That sounds like it was rough."

Derrick looked down at his coffee as the inevitable memories assailed him, of those years after high school, trying to do everything alone with no one to turn to or take comfort from.

Oh, yes, it had been rough. But the truth was, LeeAnn had been an afterthought much of the time.

He lifted his eyes with a smile. He wouldn't say any of that, of course. It was just too damn maudlin.

"No, not really." He shook his head in denial. "It was a gradual thing. No drama. No hard feelings. I actually—" He smiled ruefully, huffing a soft laugh. "She broke up with *me* when I proposed marriage while she was home for Christmas break her junior year. I had the ring and everything."

He saw Gavin wince in sympathy. Damn. He didn't want that. That wasn't the point. The point was how young and foolish and *wrong* he'd been, and how gentle and caring the breakup had been. "I offered it to her, and she got tears in her eyes. She kissed my cheek and closed my hands over it and then she told me I was trying to create a reason to hang on when it was time to accept there was nothing left and just let go. And she was absolutely right; that's *exactly* what I was doing. So she kissed me and that was that. We still send each other Christmas and birthday cards. Now LeeAnn's a successful concert violinist out in California. She's having her first baby in the spring."

He looked up and smiled at Gavin, who looked at him a bit too casually. "So you still keep in contact with her, then?"

"Just cards." He shrugged. "The occasional Facebook post. Saw her when she came home to visit her family last month."

"I think it's nice that there were no hard feelings behind it." Gavin licked his lips with a slow nod. "That you two can talk amicably like that."

"I'm sorry you can't say the same," Derrick said, his voice soft with sympathy.

Gavin shrugged, shaking his head as he held his coffee up before him. "He seemed nice enough at first. It just went downhill. Rather quickly."

"You seem the type to have something that's really intense from the get-go. Sometimes that sort of fire explodes, rather than burning out slowly."

Derrick bit his tongue the instant the words were out. Had he lost *all* control of his mouth? You didn't *say* that sort of thing on a first date.

Or maybe ever.

Gavin's voice was soft as he answered, "I suppose you're right."

"Sorry." Derrick managed not to groan. "That may have been too personal an observation."

Gavin denied it with an adamant shake of his head. "No, not at all. You see things really clearly. That's nothing to apologize for. I do throw myself headlong at things. Is that intimidating for you?"

Sweet Jesus, yes, his mind chimed in. Perhaps intimidating wasn't the right word. Whatever it was, it didn't make him feel all that safe.

He settled for a half-truth, offering Gavin a wry grin. "Not intimidating. Different, though. I've been told I move at a pace that makes snails frustrated and impatient."

Gavin smiled, and Derrick promptly lost track of what they were taking about. He was too busy looking at Gavin's mouth.

"I don't see anything wrong with being rock-steady." Gavin shrugged. "Might be a nice change of pace."

Silence fell again, not uncomfortable, but heavy with awareness. Finally Derrick pushed his empty cup aside and flagged down the waiter to ask him to close out the tab. "I should get going. But I'm glad you called me."

"So am I," Gavin said, rising and pulling on his jacket. Derrick signed his credit card slip and led the way to the door as Gavin asked, "What are your plans this weekend?"

"I'm meeting my friend Devon for pool tomorrow night, but I was hoping maybe I could come by and sand down your wall on Saturday?" he ventured hopefully.

"Sure. Maybe we could meet for lunch, and watch a movie after?" Gavin proposed as they stepped out into the parking lot. His hands twitched toward his jacket pocket, then stopped.

"That sounds good." Derrick shoved his own hands in the pockets of his leather jacket for lack of anything better to do with them. It was ridiculously cool for August.

"I'll text you, then?"

Derrick laughed. "Can't. I don't have texting on my phone. How about I call you?"

Gavin echoed the laugh as Derrick leaned against his truck, smiling. "You built your own computer and can fix every appliance known to man, but you don't have texting on your cell phone." Gavin shook his head in amusement, his hands twitching again. "It's going to be interesting, getting to know your quirks."

"Good." Derrick grinned, watching Gavin. "You okay?"

"Yeah, I just really need a cigarette, so I guess I'd better do this first." He stepped close, and Derrick's stomach thudded. Gavin's hand slid up Derrick's neck under the collar of his jacket, and his lips brushed Derrick's.

His blood pounded in his ears, and every extremity seemed to tingle as though he'd touched a poorly insulated wire. He couldn't get enough air, and he thought he understood now just what being ready to swoon must feel like.

He knew a short peck was all Gavin had in mind, but he ended up *nuzzling* Gavin, his nose stroking Gavin's ear as he breathed deep between feather-light kisses.

"*God, you smell good,*" he whispered.

Gavin gave a breathy laugh against his cheek, his arms laying over Derrick's shoulders as Derrick held lightly to his waist. "That's why I did it before the cigarette." He pulled away, his eyes soft with reluctance. "We'd better go. Call me Saturday?"

"I will." He stared at Gavin a moment, fixated on his gorgeous lips, wanting another kiss so badly his palms itched with the need to reach out. He made himself take out the keys to his truck instead, and turned away.

CHAPTER EIGHT

THERE WAS NO QUESTION that he'd call Gavin Saturday as he'd promised. He'd had to fight against the impulse to come up with a reason to do it Friday night, and his distraction had lost him another round of pool to Devon, and won him a huge heap of teasing.

Saturday morning, he managed to hold off until he'd taken the edge off his eager tension by taking Chelsea for a romp in the park and jerking off in the shower. Feeling considerably calmer in the aftermath, he dialed Gavin's number.

Gavin's voice sounded a little muzzy as he answered, despite the fact that it was nearly ten o'clock. "Hello?"

"Hi. It's Derrick."

He could hear Gavin's deep inhalation over the line, and Derrick wondered if he'd caught Gavin unprepared. "Yeah, hi. Great to hear from you. Uh, how's your morning been?"

For a moment, he imagined telling Gavin exactly what he'd done with his morning, and immediately regretted it, trying to cover his embarrassment with a chuckle and grateful Gavin couldn't actually hear him blushing over the phone.

"Been pretty good. Took my dog, Chelsea, to the park this morning. Let her run around a bit. Thought I'd give you a call, like we'd planned. I hope I didn't call too early?"

He could hear the smile in Gavin's tone. "No. Though, I might have been pretty crabby if you'd called earlier."

"Up late?" he asked, dishing up some fruit salad to eat with mozzarella cheese sticks as a snack after running around with Chelsea half the morning.

"Yeah, up late. Andi and I stayed up talking." Gavin laughed softly, and Derrick could hear dishes clanking in the background. He wondered if Gavin was only just now eating breakfast. "How about you? Did you sleep well?"

Sure, great, once I stopped thinking about Thursday night long enough to fall asleep.

"Well enough," he answered, his tone mild.

"I had a really good time the other night."

"So did I. Thanks again for calling me back."

"Did you still want to meet for lunch today?"

"I'd like that. What'd you have in mind?"

"How do you feel about Coney Islands?" Gavin asked, a grin in his tone. "I've got Netflix, we could watch a movie back at my place after you sand down the wall. That way we don't have to stay out too late, and hopefully it won't keep you away from Chelsea too long."

The lunch sounded good, but the suggestion of going back to Gavin's place to watch a movie afterward made Derrick close his eyes for a moment. Public was safe, neutral. It was different, being alone. At least it felt that way. To see where this—whatever it was—would take them outside the restraints of public decorum... he wanted that.

"I love Coneys." A hot dog loaded with mustard, onions, and a dry, meaty chili sauce probably wasn't the best idea for a date, but it sounded absolutely delicious. He'd have to remember to bring a toothbrush. "Where did you want to meet?"

There were hundreds of family-oriented diners around southeast Michigan that served Coneys as their signature dish, but not all were equal. A smile spread across his face as Gavin suggested his favorite chain. Maybe they had more in common than it had originally appeared.

"That sounds great. One-thirty?"

"Yeah, at Twelve and Main." Gavin sounded pleased. "I'll meet you there. And… I'm really looking forward to it."

"So am I." They hung up, and Derrick leaned against the counter in his kitchen, blowing out slow sigh and closing his eyes. He waited for the giddy, heady feeling to pass so he could locate his calm again. Then he laughed, digging in to his fruit salad. He'd spent more time trying to settle himself this past month than he had in the last decade. Chelsea watched him, half-curious and half-hopeful that his distraction meant he might forget the rules and decide to share his cheese. Derrick laughed, rubbing her wrinkled head.

"Don't even think about it."

He was already seated in the restaurant, two steaming cups of coffee sitting on the table, when Gavin arrived. He greeted Derrick, looking embarrassed, then excused himself quickly. When he returned from the rest room, the scent of cigarette smoke that still clung to him was fainter, masked by the scent of soap and toothpaste as he brushed past Derrick to take his seat.

Derrick looked at him a long moment, chewing the inside of his cheek thoughtfully. "Are you ashamed that you smoke?"

Gavin blinked, startled by the blunt question. "Well, yeah. Kind of a disgusting habit, wouldn't you say? At least most people think so."

Derrick shrugged. "Not my place to judge. If you're worried I'm gonna criticize, don't be. People do what they've got to do. You seem pretty considerate about not exposing other people to it. Can't ask for much more than that."

Gavin grinned. "Well, I think I rather prefer you liking the way I smell, thank you very much." He sipped his coffee, frowning slightly. "I guess I don't much like the idea that I've got this… this crutch I use, to keep myself calm or pick myself up. Especially now

79

that it's become something I have to have. I don't like anything having that sort of control over me."

"Why did you start in the first place?"

"Back in college, studying all night. I lived on coffee and cigarettes. Also, by that time I had quit dancing and I was putting on a little more weight and smoking helped keep that down. I had almost managed to quit until about a year ago. Living with someone who is a heavy smoker makes it really hard to stop."

"You're a dancer?" Derrick's eyebrows rose, and suddenly that odd fluidity he'd noticed in Gavin's movements made sense.

Gavin nodded. "Used to be. It started out just with some basic ballet classes when I was young. My mom was a bit of an east coast socialite, also, and made sure I got some ballroom training, too. Which I really liked. I did that until I graduated high school."

"Why'd you stop?"

Gavin shrugged. "I originally made dance my minor at college, and I was actually really good, but I wasn't good enough that I would ever be able to do it professionally. Then I had an injury and couldn't practice, and I needed more time to study, so I just decided it was time to stop."

"That seems a shame."

Gavin shook his head. "Maybe it would have been, if I'd given it up to do something I didn't enjoy, but like I said, I really actually like what I do, so I'm okay with it. And, I dunno, maybe some day I'll take it up again, at least on a casual basis, or for exercise." He grinned. "It would solve the dilemma I have of not wanting to go out jogging in the winter, at least."

Derrick smiled as the waitress approached.

"Glad to know you have good taste in Coneys," Gavin murmured after they'd ordered.

"Can't get a Coney without onions. I'm pretty sure there are laws against it. Maybe even Commandments."

Derrick's smile widened as Gavin laughed aloud, and then the ball was in Gavin's court.

"So you're, what, thirty?" Gavin asked.

"Thirty-one." He pushed his hair back from his face. "I guess that brings me to asking your age."

"I'm twenty-eight." Gavin chuckled, flashing him another grin full of mischief. "Have to say, I like that whole idea of the *older man*."

Shit. He let his hair slip out from behind his ear in an effort to hide the blush. The attention of other people was a large part of why he kept his social circle so small. He saw lots of clients, of course, but usually they just pointed him in the direction of whatever he needed to work on and left him to it. They didn't scrutinize him like Gavin was doing, watching for each reaction.

"Now you're just trying to embarrass me," Derrick accused, and Gavin laughed.

"Perhaps."

The arrival of their food provided a welcome distraction, especially because he had started to feel the first hints of shakiness indicating he'd gone too long without eating. Perhaps he should have had more of that fruit and cheese earlier.

He refused to let himself think too hard, as he followed Gavin back to his place after lunch. Gavin stepped out to the balcony for another cigarette as Derrick began sanding the patched drywall smooth. After they'd each finished, Gavin went thought his ritual of washing his hands and brushing his teeth, then offered Derrick beer and sat down to scroll through the video streaming options on Netflix.

He didn't much care about the movie they chose. If anything, he deliberately showed the most interest in the movies that would be the least engrossing. That way, it wouldn't matter if he and Gavin turned their attention to conversation. If Gavin realized the scheme, he played along, and after the phony repairs, Derrick felt no remorse for that tiny bit of well-intentioned manipulation.

Gavin sat just far enough away to not be invading Derrick's space, but not so far that he seemed to be avoiding contact. Derrick hesitated a moment, drawing a deep breath and stopping an internal debate before it began, and shifted an inch or two closer to the middle of the sofa. He didn't really know what to *do* with the tension thrumming through him, the awareness of Gavin only a few inches away. Or perhaps it was more honest to say he knew what he wanted to do, he just wasn't sure he could, or should, bring himself to do it. He was limited not only by his own shyness, but the foreign and unfamiliar notion of being with another person without all the childish fits and starts and torturously slow fumbling that had comprised his only other experience so many years ago.

He wanted Gavin. It was just that simple. And he was pretty damn certain Gavin wanted him, too. His understanding that the proper, smart thing to do would be to take things slow, to learn about Gavin, to become friends, clashed against more than ten years of abstinence and a sexual awareness too strong to be denied.

When Derrick turned his head, Gavin's whiskey-colored eyes and beautiful mouth were *right there*.

He didn't want a hesitant, inch-by-inch approach. In utter contradiction of everything he thought he'd ever known about himself, he just wanted to let go and plunge headlong into this. He felt as though if he could just barrel past the uncertainty, if he could just feel Gavin's hands on him, *truly* on him, all the questions and anxiety would just fade away and everything would be *right*.

He could do it, he thought, swallowing hard. He was right there on the brink of it. He had it in him to make that move after all, Derrick realized. He could turn and pull Gavin into a kiss *right now* and things would move on from that and there wouldn't be any more doubt. It would be a relief for both of them.

In the end, it wasn't his fears, but the knowledge of existing complications—at least on Gavin's end—which stopped Derrick. The timing was bad, he'd said. So Derrick would wait, and let him take the lead no matter how much his body screamed to take more direct action.

He and his hands were good friends for a reason. He drew a deep breath and pushed away the impulse to escalate matters.

If things never went any further than that intoxicating brush of a kiss they'd had the other night, so be it.

He didn't catch another word of the movie. All his awareness was hyper-focused on Gavin's hand, which had come to rest on his knee, his thumb stroking *almost* unintentionally, making it impossible for Derrick *not* to be conscious of the touch. He moved closer, silently requesting more contact, encouraging Gavin not to be so hesitant but leaving the ball in his court.

When the movie ended, Derrick found himself irritated with it for doing so. Now he'd have to go home, and that one touch would haunt him for days, or weeks, or however long it took for one of them to work themselves up to trying this again.

When Gavin hesitantly proposed that Derrick stay and have dinner with him, Derrick accepted.

Cooking dinner with someone was a novelty. Not that they did anything different than when he and Devon barbecued together, but still, it *was* different. They worked in tandem preparing the food in the kitchen before taking it out to the balcony, and it felt intimate somehow. The awareness that still charged the air between them made every passing brush, every exchange, no matter how light-hearted and chatty, somehow *more*.

"You cook for yourself a lot?" Gavin asked, leaning against the railing of the balcony as Derrick grilled the steaks. He'd been fascinated by the herb rub Derrick had made for them and insisted on getting the recipe.

"Pretty much all the time. I could eat out if I wanted to, but I'm a bit of a tightwad, really. Which is why I do things like use an ancient cell phone without texting and repair appliances that I should have retired twenty years ago. I cook my own meals and take leftovers for lunch. I don't tend to eat out unless it's a social thing."

"I really should do the same, but I've discovered I hate cooking for one. When it's for company, I really enjoy it, but when it's just me, I can't seem to make myself care."

Derrick shrugged uncomfortably, wondering why he felt awkward discussing his solitary existence. Would Gavin think he was boring? Or pathetic? "I guess I just got used to it, over the years."

He didn't protest when Gavin insisted he didn't want Derrick driving after the two beers he'd had with dinner. Two beers with food weren't enough to impair him, but he was plenty happy to play along and return to the sofa. When Gavin chose a sitcom to watch, Derrick suspected he'd done it for the same reason Derrick had chosen the movie, picking something they could easily ignore.

And when Gavin leaned his head on Derrick's shoulder, light and tentative, he was sure of it. Gavin still smelled incredible. His cologne and shampoo combined with the lingering essence of beer and steak. Even the faint hint of underlying tobacco didn't detract from it.

As he had earlier, Derrick reined in the impulse to escalate things. He knew nothing about the previous relationship Gavin had been in. Physical attraction hummed and snapped between them like electric currents arcing through the air; the constant tingling buzz made it impossible to think of anything else but his determination to let Gavin move at whatever pace worked for him.

And why was he suddenly scared? Why did the idea of putting his arm around Gavin—which seemed to be what Gavin had invited him to do—and simply being close to him frighten Derrick far more than the thought of kissing him?

Because in kissing Gavin, or groping him, or hell, even going to bed with him, Derrick could convince himself it was just lust. Nothing more than hormones and too many years of abstinence. A good time with nothing else at stake. Snuggling could mean something else. Something that involved way more than he felt sure about permitting just yet.

It wasn't the idea of sex that scared him. He could handle that, and he could handle just being friends. It was the somewhere in between, where feelings could happen, that he wasn't sure about.

But Gavin felt good against him. *Right.* Closing his eyes for a moment, Derrick drew a slow breath and laid his arm over Gavin's shoulders, silently inviting him to make himself comfortable. And Gavin did, slipping down a little to make more room for Derrick's arm, laying his head against Derrick's chest, where his heart hammered within the too-tight confines of his ribs.

Derrick had no clue what show they were watching. He couldn't hear over the drumming in his ears and he didn't want to even look at the screen, nor could he stop glancing down at Gavin's hair just below his chin. It took all Derrick's willpower to keep himself from leaning down and nuzzling his face in Gavin's hair to try to get a better whiff of him.

When Gavin lifted his head and tilted it back to look at him, Derrick's eyes immediately went to Gavin's lips. His fingers tightened on Gavin's shoulder and when he finally managed to tear his eyes away from Gavin's mouth to meet his gaze, he knew Gavin had seen the stare.

And then Gavin wet his lips with his tongue.

Derrick caught a nervous breath, torn between the impulse to *act* and that tiny, nagging hint of uncertainty that maybe Gavin wasn't ready for that yet.

Gavin smiled, looking faintly amused. "You really don't know an invitation when you see one, do you?"

"Guess I don't. Look," he said haltingly as he tried to form his racing thoughts into words that would actually be intelligible when he spoke them. "You know, it's been a while. And I don't really know what I should do here. What you need."

Gavin looked up at him a while longer, his eyes wide, pupils large and dark, before he pushed himself up. He pulled his glasses off, his movement slow and deliberate as he laid them on the coffee table, giving Derrick plenty of time to back out. Then Gavin turned and kissed him.

Derrick heard himself moan, his arm tightening behind Gavin, sliding down to wrap around his back and draw him closer. He tasted as good as he smelled, even the hint of beer on his breath. It was strange; fulfilling the promise of contact that had been hovering between them all day both relieved Derrick's tension and made it ten times worse. It threatened to send something ravenous to the surface that he hadn't known lurked beneath.

The touch of Gavin's hand on his face, stroking his cheek and jaw, felt good. Gavin's cool fingers against his skin both soothed Derrick's nerves and brought them snapping to attention. And when they moved down to Derrick's neck it was even better. Derrick gasped into the kiss at that touch on his sensitive skin. As his mouth opened on the inhalation, he felt Gavin's tongue against his lips.

Oh, sweet Jesus....

Any thought he had of taking things slow promptly dissipated. He wanted Gavin's body against his, and they shifted simultaneously. Derrick turned as much as he could without drawing his legs up onto the sofa, and Gavin drew his knees under him, the motion giving him a height advantage that he used to take control of the kiss. His hand buried itself in Derrick's hair, his mouth covered Derrick's. His lips urged Derrick's open, his tongue sliding in, stroking.

Derrick's other arm came around Gavin, trying to draw him even closer. He wasn't sure how Gavin ended up in his lap, straddling his hips. Gavin loomed over him with a hiss of denim-on-denim as Derrick, without any thought or intention, shifted beneath him, seeking friction against the hard-on trapped beneath his fly.

"God, yes…"

He didn't know he'd spoken, panting the words between increasingly urgent kisses. He rolled his hips again beneath Gavin, beyond self-consciousness, not *caring* if it was too forward, too suggestive. Gavin didn't seem to mind; his own body moved to increase the pressure. As that first kiss had done for his nerves, the rubbing of Gavin's cock against his beneath the layers of denim both soothed the insistent, throbbing ache in Derrick's balls and made it far more desperate. He groaned, his hands clutching at Gavin's back, the kisses passing beyond *exploratory* and heading straight into *demanding*.

When Gavin's hands closed in his hair, gripping it, Derrick arched his spine, his hips lifting as he responded to the pressure drawing his head back. The pull on his hair was tight, good, skirting the edge of uncomfortable in an absolutely perfect way. He tore his mouth away from Gavin's with a whimper as the pull became harder; overwhelmed, he tried to catch a panting breath and get a grip. With every response, every sensation, Derrick felt closer to the brink of flying completely, insanely out of control.

"Sorry," Gavin murmured as his hands released Derrick's hair and Derrick almost groaned at the loss. He shook his head in silent denial as his brain tried to remember how to make words.

"No… no… no need."

Abandoning any further attempt at speech, he pulled Gavin back to him, taking over the kiss. Hard, urgent, edging toward rough as he tried to find an outlet for that plaguing need for *more*. He was aware, now, of the rise and fall of his hips, knowing full well what it suggested. He wanted Gavin. God, he wanted him, and just the *wanting* felt intoxicating. He was high, beyond thought or reason, doubt or control.

More, his body demanded, gripping fistfuls of the back of Gavin's shirt, thrusting up against Gavin.

More. Gavin responded, pressing down to meet him.

Derrick leaned back, reclining as far as he could against the sofa, no more concerned with the message he sent by moving toward the horizontal than with the blatant grinding of his hips against Gavin. He drew Gavin down tighter above him, picking up the pace, rubbing against him urgently. The delirious thought occurred to him that he should be thankful he'd jerked off that morning, or this would already be over.

He didn't want it to be over. Not nearly over. He wanted... God, he wanted Gavin's skin. It didn't occur to him to ask first; his hands simply obeyed the imperative without thought or hesitation, releasing their grip on Gavin's shirt at the shoulders to seize it lower, pulling it up.

The way Gavin's body tensed didn't register, not at first, even when Gavin drew back and panted, "Oh, God. Wait... wait."

For a moment there was no comprehension, beyond the fact that Gavin's mouth no longer moved against his, that the friction of Gavin's cock no longer ground against his own. It was gone, and he wanted it back. He was moving for Gavin again, seeking his lips, when the words finally penetrated.

"Wh—what is it? Have I...?" He became aware of his hands clutching Gavin's shirt, pulling it up. His stomach sank. The mindless *wanting* faded into the background as rational thought returned. His balls throbbed with agonizing insistence even as mortification set in.

He'd gone too far. Gavin didn't want this.

"Oh. Sorry. Sorry." He let go of Gavin's shirt, trying to sit up, queasy with humiliated rejection. "Sorry."

"Um, no. No, it's not you. God." He wasn't sure if it was any consolation or not that Gavin looked as tortured by the sudden halt as Derrick felt. His dick was still painfully hard within his jeans, a condition that was only marginally improved when Gavin shifted off his lap, relieving some of the pressure.

Gavin took a moment, futilely trying to straighten his clothing as though it would help him organize his thoughts. "I need to tell you something. Before this goes any further. *If* it does."

"Okay." Derrick pushed himself back up to sitting, raking his hair back from his face and pushing it behind his ear. He forced his thoughts away from the desire to get back to what they'd been doing. Gavin sounded far too solemn for that.

He blew out a calming breath. "Okay. Say what you gotta say, then."

It seemed to take Gavin forever to answer. The longer he stared at the floor without meeting Derrick's eyes, the more apprehensive Derrick became, his gut sinking in fear.

Gavin's voice was halted and shook when he finally spoke. "Um, I've mentioned that my last relationship wasn't, uh, wasn't the best." Derrick nodded, even though Gavin wasn't looking at him, willing Gavin to continue. "He refused to find out his status. His... his, um, HIV status. And I didn't know that until it was too late."

The temperature in the room seemed to plummet. His skin prickled with cold sweat. Derrick felt himself shutting down. His mind, even his body seemed to go so numb he might as well have been dunked in Lake Huron in January. His emotions fled, leaving him empty. Those glorious moments of feeling *everything* bled away into feeling absolutely nothing.

He stared at Gavin, not really seeing him. A dull mantra pounded at brain like a drumbeat.

I knew it. I knew it.

Yes, he'd known it was a bad idea to get involved with anyone, but he'd chosen to do it anyway. He had no one but his own fool self to blame for that. He shut the chiding voice up, closed it off. He turned Gavin's words over in his head methodically. He dissected and analyzed them dispassionately, his face blank.

When he spoke, his voice was flat. Empty.

"You. You, um. You didn't take precautions, I take it?"

Gavin flinched, looking away a split second after something haunting made his eyes go distant and unfocused. "Not always. It wasn't what I wanted. Not really. It's… it's complicated."

Derrick gave a slow nod. He took his time examining that, measuring out the passage of seconds in the thunderous beating of his pulse in his ears. Gavin's voice sounded far away, nearly lost in the cacophony.

Again, an inflectionless voice he barely recognized as his own spoke.

"So. You said you didn't know until it was too late. You've, um… tested…." A small surge of emotion, *pain*, tried to pierce the void. He shoved it aside and buried it in favor of that protective stillness. "You've tested positive, then?"

"No," Gavin said with an emphatic shake of his head. "I still have about four months until I… until I can say with absolute certainty I'm not positive. But I haven't tested positive yet. My doctor says at over two months since last exposure, that's a really good sign. Usually it shows up within one to three months. It doesn't often take as long as six, but it can."

"Four months." He sat with that, silent, and Gavin let him. Anger, unreasoning and unreasonable, began to nibble at the edges of that numb, detached feeling.

"Why?" The word came out hard and sharp, more a demand than a question.

Gavin started, frowning in confusion. "Why…?"

Why didn't you tell me before I was ready to go to bed with you? Why did you ever start flirting with me in the first place? Why did you call me back when I was ready to let go of this idea and move on? Why were you so foolish?

"That's an awful lot of trust to put in someone. Why didn't you *make* him get tested, show you proof? Why'd you take that risk?" His mouth curled in a small sneer, and he knew it was ugly and cynical and judgmental, but he couldn't make himself stop.

90

"No, wait. Let me guess. You just loved him *that* much, it was worth risking your life."

He regretted the accusation immediately as Gavin flinched. Shit. It wasn't his place to judge Gavin's choices. He swallowed down the knee-jerk anger, groping around in his head to try to find that frigid calm again.

"And if I hadn't said anything, tell me, would you have let yourself get carried away?" Gavin shot back. "Because it certainly felt like it."

So much for trying to quell his bitterness.

Derrick's voice hardened again. "I was well on my way to sleeping with you, if that's what you're asking. But I damn sure wouldn't have done it without a rubber. Would have insisted on us both wearing 'em. Sorry, Gav, but two dates? No. Much as I like you, no."

He didn't let himself examine whether or not that was completely truthful. The fact was, it hadn't occurred to him to buy condoms and bring them with him. He was nearly certain that he would have remembered to ask Gavin if he had them, but maybe not one hundred percent.

Gavin's scowled. "I don't have to justify a *thing* to you, Derrick, but if you want to know, it wasn't the first time I was with him. I'm smarter than that, if not by much. We were together for a year. A year is a lot of time for trust to build." He grimaced. "*Misplaced* trust, but it is what it is."

Stop being an asshole, man.

He couldn't seem to check himself. The throbbing pain at his temples wasn't helping, either. He hated the anger, hated the fear making him lash out. The nothingness was better, but that seemed to have abandoned him.

"Trust. Right." He had to move, surging to his feet to pace restlessly before turning to look at Gavin again. "I could ask just what sort of *trust* leaves a guy white as a sheet when he looks at a text message, what kind of *trust* punches holes in his walls, but I

91

guess that's none of my business." He moved to the sliding balcony door, bracing a fist on the glass next to his head and staring out without seeing anything. A hint of movement in Gavin's reflection and the sound of the refrigerator opening and bottles clinking told him Gavin had grabbed another beer for himself.

Derrick wished he could do the same.

Gavin's voice, when he answered the charge, was soft. Ashamed. "I said it was misplaced."

The bitterness bled away, and in its place came sorrow. That was even worse. He wouldn't let himself feel that. Not again. Not ever, ever again.

He didn't know how long he stood there, systematically replacing grief with nothingness. He did it with slow, methodical precision. He tackled it with the same careful accuracy he'd dedicated to building Gavin's shelves. A small eternity lapsed, filled with endless, echoing silence. Gavin still stood in the kitchen, waiting. He knew it, and he knew Gavin was hurt, and afraid, and a hundred other things Derrick didn't want him to feel, a hundred things that made every instinct in him yearn to comfort and protect.

But there was nothing he could do for Gavin. Not without destroying all the stability he'd worked so hard to build.

Minutes ticked by as he stared unseeingly out the patio door. He knew what he needed to do, but he absolutely didn't want to do that. He didn't want to take that irrevocable step that would push Gavin, and whatever might have happened between them, away forever.

Finally, he drew a breath to speak, the emptiness in his chest beginning to ache.

"I want you to know, I'm not...." He hesitated, clearing his throat against the tight, choked sound of his own voice. He knew he owed Gavin an explanation but be couldn't bring himself to put it in any sort of terms that would make it any more palatable. Not without telling Gavin things he couldn't bring himself to say, things he wanted to leave far in the past. "Look, I keep myself informed. I know how to be safe. I don't have any irrational fear that makes me think I can't... breathe the same air or some ignorant bullshit like that. It's not prejudice, I swear. I just...."

God, why was this so difficult? He hardly knew Gavin; it shouldn't be this hard to walk away. He turned to meet Gavin's hopeless eyes, swallowing hard as he pushed away memories and grief. "I can't."

Shoving himself away from the patio door, refusing to let himself pause or falter, he grabbed his keys, heading for the hallway that would lead him out the door.

He paused at the entrance to the hallway, looking at Gavin a final time. "There're reasons I've been alone all this time." He saw the stunned look dawn upon Gavin's face as he began to comprehend that Derrick was leaving, and that ache in his chest grew tighter.

"Thanks for the really good time. I like you, Gav. A lot. I'm sorry. I just can't."

Hanging his head, unable to meet Gavin's eyes any longer, he walked without stopping to the door and closed it behind him.

In the elevator, he pushed the stop button between floors, grinding the heels of his hands against his eyes. When he felt he could be calm again, he restarted the elevator, letting it take him down to his truck.

CHAPTER NINE

DERRICK DROVE HOME with his white-knuckled hands gripping the steering wheel, trying not to shake.

Fuck.

Fuck.

His pulse raced, heart pounding. His breath came short and rapid, as though he'd just finished a long sprint. Nausea churned in his gut, made worse by the bitter tang of adrenalin souring his breath.

He'd had enough anxiety attacks by now to be familiar with the feeling, but this was shaping up to be the worst he'd had in years. If it kept up, he wouldn't be able to drive. He tried to tamp down the feeling, though he knew it was a futile effort. Full dark had fallen; it wasn't safe to pull to the side of the road. His only hope was to get home quickly, before it got worse.

The anxiety mounted as he arrived home, and Chelsea came dashing out the dog door to greet him through the fence around the back yard. He paused only to fill Chelsea's food dish, ignoring her disappointment that he didn't acknowledge or pet her, before heading into the bedroom. On the top of the dresser was a small, antique clock that had been a wedding present when his grandparents had gotten married.

He opened the door that gave access to the gears within and, from the small space beneath the clockworks, withdrew a small bag of marijuana.

Six months before her death, Derrick had begun risking arrest to acquire marijuana for his grandmother. She'd protested at first, but the only other option had been dangerous levels of opiate painkillers. Gram hadn't wanted her mind dulled in those final months, especially when his Gramps had been on such a rapid decline with his Alzheimer's.

The weed had helped. She'd continued to use it until after Gramps had died and she'd had her final Christmas with Derrick. After that, her final few weeks were spent in a drugged daze, barely aware of Derrick and the hospice nurse who came to help take care of her.

The year after her death, Derrick began to experience anxiety attacks. He saw a therapist for a while, but she didn't tell him anything he didn't already know. All she wanted him to do was wallow in memories, and he refused to do that. Instead, he'd done some research and found that in other states, medical marijuana was being used to treat anxiety disorders, without the potential side effects of antidepressants and anti-anxiety medications. When Michigan finally passed their medical marijuana act, he got his license. Coping with the attacks since had been easier.

Thankful that the next day was Sunday, he sat in an armchair in the corner of the bedroom, tamping the grass into a small pipe and lighting it. If he'd had to work the next day, he wouldn't have allowed himself to smoke. The effects never lingered that long, but he still made certain not to take any chances. If he had a particularly bad attack during the week, he rescheduled his jobs for the next day.

The marijuana calmed the racing of his heart and shortness of breath. The gut-twisting sense of falling started to abate. He stopped once he felt steadier, well before he began to get high. He put the pipe aside and, leaning his head against the back of his chair, closed his eyes.

With calm came a hollow feeling of regret. Regret for the lost opportunity of—whatever had been developing between Gavin and himself. Regret that he'd never know what it might have become. Regret that the short period of excitement was over and now he'd have to go back to the way things had been and find a way to live within his old routine.

Regret that he'd walked away.

He wasn't used to having regrets. It wasn't a comfortable feeling. He'd always known what he wanted, what was right for him. He took his time, reached his decisions with slow, careful deliberation, and once he'd decided, he moved forward without hesitation.

He didn't look back.

I shouldn't have left.

The thought nagged him as he mechanically showered and brushed his teeth, and gave Chelsea a few perfunctory pets before climbing into bed. She lay beside the bed, opting to remain close to him rather than sleeping in her dog bed in the corner of the living room. As the hours passed without rest, Derrick rolled onto his stomach and hung his arm over the side of the bed, stroking her short, sleek fur. His thoughts continued to churn just short of the panic he felt before.

I shouldn't have left.

He lay there with that one thought haunting him until an early dawn lightened the August sky. He spent Sunday on the sofa, Chelsea hovering watchfully nearby, not paying attention to the Tigers game. Staring at the television without really seeing it, he tried to fit the events of the past week into the context of his everyday life and make sense of it.

Why had he ever let himself be attracted to Gavin in the first place? It wasn't like him. He'd gotten so used to shutting down any hint of interest he might feel toward another person that to do so was second nature. He didn't ignore the attraction he felt for other people; he simply never let himself feel attraction to begin with.

Why now? Why Gavin? Of all people, why Gavin?

It made no sense in the pattern of the life he'd built. It went contrary to everything Derrick had made of himself over the last decade.

He had several beers and went to bed for another restless night filled with too many thoughts.

He was better off out of the situation, he decided somewhere in the middle of the night. With that resolve, he pushed the nagging voice of regret to the back of his mind. What had happened was a fluke, an aberration. Now he could put it behind him as a lesson learned and get back to the life that made sense to him.

Groggy from lack of sleep, he rose and went about his morning routine with robotic precision.

The familiarity and organization of it all was wrong. Empty. Uninteresting. Had it always felt this way? The last month, he'd felt more alive, more awake, than he had in his entire adult life. What he had always known no longer seemed to be enough, now that he was aware there was *more*. But *more* included risk; terrifying, unpredictable, uncontrollable risk.

Which is the entire point, dumbass, he scoffed at himself as he loaded up his truck. *You're better off playing it safe.*

He'd been just fine, these last ten years, without those sorts of complications. Forget LeeAnn and her view-from-the-gallery advice. Who was she to waltz in after only seeing him a few times over a decade and assess the way he should be living? He had friends, he had activities, he had hobbies and interests and a job he enjoyed. He had a life he *liked*.

Why didn't that feel like it was enough anymore?

But the *risk*....

He knew it wasn't like when he'd been a kid, first learning about the spectre of AIDS on the evening news his parents and grandparents had watched. HIV was no longer an automatic short-term death sentence. These days, HIV positive people, with the right medications and lifestyle, had a life expectancy that wasn't far below the average.

But he also knew there were strains of HIV that were drug-resistant and virulent, progressing rapidly to AIDS.

And he knew that AIDS was an ugly way to die.

The thought of watching Gavin die threatened to trigger another anxiety attack. He couldn't think about it.

It was strange, he thought, as he pulled out of the driveway and headed for the lumberyard. His own safety wasn't even a concern. He knew he'd be conscientious about using protection, and he knew Gavin would be, also, despite whatever had happened with his ex. He didn't doubt it for an instant.

That wasn't the issue. It wasn't what kept him from obeying the nagging voice inside which told him to call Gavin. It wouldn't be silenced, despite his resolve. It told him to apologize and beg Gavin to meet for coffee so they could talk things over.

But he couldn't do it. He *couldn't*.

He was better off, he reminded himself. Better off alone than involved in something messy. Something risky.

Mustering a placid if insincere smile, he paid the clerk and went outside to wait by his truck.

Miss Ingrid was not a paying client.

She lived just down the block in the neighborhood of nearly identical red-brick houses Derrick lived in, and she had been his grandmother's closest friend for over forty years. She and Gram had met twice a week for coffee and gin rummy. Her husband had died when Derrick was sixteen, and Gram had asked him, as a favor to her, to do some repairs and maintenance around Miss Ingrid's house.

He'd never stopped. He'd repaired her appliances, used his contractor's discount to get her wholesale pricing to replace things when needed, rebuilt her bathroom floor after a leak had caused it to rot out, and installed her carpet. And he'd never charged her a cent for labor.

When her eyesight got too poor for her to drive, he began taking her to the grocery store once a week. She, in turn, repaid him with occasional batches of amazing Swedish baked goods. If there was one person left in this world beside Devon who was the next-best-thing to family for Derrick, she was that person.

This year she needed new shingles on her roof before the fall rains began. The next time she'd have to have her entire roof replaced, and he'd have to arrange for another contractor, one with an actual crew, to do the work. But this job he could do by himself.

As lumberyard employees loaded his truck with packs of shingles, he realized, in her mid-eighties already, odds were high Miss Ingrid would never need to have her whole roof replaced.

Shit.

Working up on the roof forced Derrick not to get lost in his own thoughts. He had to concentrate or risk injury. Smashing his thumb with a hammer was the least of his worries when he could take a twelve-foot fall and break his neck. Though August turned out to be cooler than usual, working in the open sun was still brutal, and he made a point of coming down frequently for plenty of water and time to cool off before climbing back up. It wasn't safe to think, and so he didn't. He worked until nearly sundown, when the darkening sky made it impossible to continue. Then he came down, ate the dinner Miss Ingrid insisted on making for him, and drove back home to shower and collapse in bed, too weary to think.

That got him through to Wednesday evening, when he finally finished Miss Ingrid's roof.

"You've been quiet this week," she said, sitting at the table with a cup of after-dinner coffee while Derrick was still eating. Her face was deeply wrinkled, and her eyes were the most amazing shade of dark blue Derrick had ever seen. Her skin had a fine, luminescent quality that confirmed for him the gorgeous young

100

woman in the black and white photos lining her hallway walls was her. "Well, quieter than usual, at least. It has always been hard to drag words out of you."

She might require a walker to get around some days, but her mind was still as keen as the day he'd first met her fifteen years ago.

"Yeah," Derrick muttered, swallowing the last of the delicious stuffed cabbage rolls and gravy. "I've been busy. Lot on my mind."

"Trouble with a girl?" A hint of fond amusement colored her lightly accented voice.

Anyone else, he would have shut down and told them not to ask personal questions, but not Miss Ingrid. Even before he'd moved in with his grandparents, he'd been raised with an old-fashioned, deferential respect for his elders, and Miss Ingrid in particular merited it. Derrick liked her too well to bring himself to be so blunt with her. So he let her pry, knowing she didn't do it often. She never pushed, and she never did so just to be nosy. She was concerned about him, and he felt he owed it to her to allow her that.

Still, he wasn't ready to talk about it. He wasn't sure he'd ever be.

"No." He shook his head, wiping his mouth with one of her fine cloth napkins. Whenever he came to dinner, she treated him like Important Company, serving the meal on her best china and table linens. No matter how many times he reassured her it wasn't necessary, she insisted.

Bah! Humor an old woman who doesn't get company much these days!

"No, Miss Ingrid. Got nothing to do with a girl."

"Trouble with a boy?" Derrick choked mid-sip as he drank water out of a crystal goblet, coughing and staring at her with wide, watering eyes as she dropped a wicked wink.

She waved a dismissive hand at his spluttering discomfiture, her amusement subsiding a little. Then she reached over and squeezed his hand. "I know about such things. *Love*—even the sort of love that makes others raise their eyebrows—is not a modern invention."

Derrick blushed, ducking his head. "Miss Ingrid, I...."

She leaned back, looking at him with affection and sipping her coffee. "You do not have to talk if you do not want to. I am being a meddling old biddy and I know it. I simply wished to make it known that if you did, you will not find me shocked or disgusted as you would so many others my age."

Derrick looked down at his empty plate, his heart racing with the feeling of being put on the spot, exposed for all the world to see. It wasn't true, and he knew it, but that didn't stop his deep-rooted sense of privacy from cringing in agony.

"How did you know?" he asked softly. He didn't talk about personal issues with people. He *liked* his privacy. But now, an unfamiliar yearning settled in his chest, to share his burdens with someone who might understand. He couldn't talk with Devon; the HIV issue would concern him deeply. Some of the kids he worked to get off the streets, even at such a young age, were HIV positive. He'd be far too concerned for Derrick's safety to give Gavin any sort of reasonable chance.

She shrugged, serene as she sipped her coffee. "I didn't. It was merely a lucky guess. You have been too much alone, all these years since your grandparents passed on. You have not brought any girls home, which I thought perhaps meant you were being... discreet."

He shook his head in adamant denial at the implication he'd been living in the closet. "No. No. I have been alone. This is all new. Really, *really* new. And it's... there's problems."

"He does not feel as you do?" Miss Ingrid rose and poured him a cup of coffee as he pushed his plate away.

Derrick snorted, picking up his cup. "If I had the first clue what I was feeling, maybe I could answer that. No. That's not it."

She tilted her head, staring at him over the rim of her cup without speaking, not asking the obvious question.

He blurted out the answer anyway. "He could be sick. And I'm not sure I could handle that. Not again."

"Ah." Miss Ingrid bowed her head, and her lips moved silently for a moment. Derrick knew she was murmuring a short prayer for the souls of his departed grandparents.

She, more than anyone, knew what those years from the time he was eighteen to the time he was twenty-one had been like. She'd been the one to take over the care of his grandparents for an hour or two here and there, pushing him out the door when he became overwhelmed. It had been Miss Ingrid he'd turned to for advice when, not long after he turned twenty, he had broken down, muffling sobs with his fist in the basement one day because he could no longer cope with caring for both of them full-time. Finally, ashamed and defeated for not being able to handle it alone, he'd hired a nurse at her urging, to help so that he could give himself a break by working. His choice to start his own business had followed. It had been the result of a decision to keep his hours flexible so that he could continue to take care of his grandparents, and that, too, had been her idea.

Miss Ingrid had been there for the funerals for his grandparents, and then two years later, for Derrick's brother's when he'd died in Iraq. From a discreet distance, in her quiet, kind way, she'd watched him recover from the exhaustion and hopelessness of those years. With her encouragement, he'd built himself back up after each and every loss.

"All love carries a risk," she said finally, looking up.

He nodded, swallowing. "I—I know that. I'm just not sure I'm up for taking on that sort of risk."

"You would rather remain alone?" Her voice lifted incredulously, and Derrick shrugged with a small smile. No one ever seemed to understand why he, or anyone, would *want* to be alone.

103

Instead of trying to explain, he drawled with exaggerated Southern charm, "Well, now, ma'am, who could be lonely with a pretty girl like you just down the block?"

She laughed, blushing in spite of herself. "Your flattery won't work on me, young man! Set your sights on someone your own age!"

Then she sobered, giving him a knowing look that said she both knew he had evaded the question and that she wouldn't push it if he didn't want to answer.

Derrick shrugged awkwardly under her regard. "Being alone's worked for me this long. Don't see any reason why it shouldn't still."

Miss Ingrid frowned. "Some people are made to be alone. Others, I think, are not. I suppose no one but you can say which group you belong to. I would think it would be hard, to have a taste of something, and then give it up again."

Derrick looked away. "Better that than getting involved in something I just can't deal with, or letting someone rely on me when I can't…."

"But then you rob yourself of moments of joy you might have had." She sighed, and patted his hand. "Stay here."

She left and came back with one of the framed arrays of photos that hung in her hallway. She laid it on the table beside his empty plate, pointing. Derrick looked closely at the blurry old photograph. He recognized the beautiful teenage girl as Miss Ingrid, but not the plainer, more severe-looking girl she stood beside.

"That is Vilma. In this picture I was perhaps fourteen? And she was seventeen. She was my girlhood friend. When my parents died, her family welcomed me to live with them and help with their farm. We spent every day together. We walked to school together, we did our chores together. Hers was a small house, so we shared a room, slept in the same bed. We were never apart.

"No one knew, of course, what we did. How we felt. In our day one would never discuss such a thing. There was no thought of us spending our lives together. We knew we would be expected to find husbands and live as other women, and while she might have been brave enough to defy that convention, I was not. I think her parents began to suspect. When the Soviets bombed our town—they claimed it was an accident, but they had a couple of such "accidents" during the war—our home was irreparably damaged. Her parents decided to take her with them to live with other relatives in Stockholm, and they made it clear that I was not welcome to come. From the age of sixteen on, I had to make my own way. I never told anyone. Not the other women in my life for whom I felt… something. Not even Josef, God rest his soul."

"I'm sorry, Miss Ingrid. Sorry that happened to you. Sorry you had to… live that way. I'm sorry."

"I did not tell you for your pity," she snapped. She pulled the picture frame away almost protectively and laid it on the other end of the table. "I do not regret a single day of what happened. I do not even regret losing her, or never finding her again. The separation was painful, but inevitable. What mattered was the time we had together. Those are the memories I cherish. For a short time as a young woman, I had something beautiful and precious and thrilling. Something I would never have in quite the same way again. Something which taught me who I was. Whatever happened after, even the loss, my life would be less if I had not had that. On the day I die, my only regret would be if I hadn't had it. If I had been too much a coward to take it while I had the chance."

Derrick swallowed hard, toying with the handle of his coffee cup. "I don't think I'm as brave as you, ma'am."

She shrugged, her expression understanding, but not necessarily approving. "That is the choice for you to make, of course. You will avoid sorrow, certainly, but you will also deprive yourself of joy. For as long as I've known you—except perhaps

105

those horrible years when your grandparents were ill—you've been a very complacent young man. Your grandmother once told me you were the still waters that run deep, and so you are. Always calm and serene; never a complaint or even a bad mood. You go out of your way to take care of others even when it means depriving yourself. You need little and ask for nothing. Your life is a peaceful one, but I'm not sure it's a happy one. Only you can say, of course, but I have seen your home. You live surrounded by the past and think little of the future. And perhaps that is all you need. If you feel contentment is enough for you, then take that if it is what you want. Just ask yourself, when you are my age and looking back on your life—what will your regrets be? And do you fear them more?"

Did he?

None of the rest of his jobs that week were as demanding as Miss Ingrid's shingles. Mostly he handled minor repair jobs. A furnace that needed to be replaced before winter. A garage door opener and garbage disposal installed. Doors hung. Baseboards replaced.

He worked with his customary mild-mannered professionalism, offering his clients a mellow smile and a polite handshake. But the work left him far too much time to think.

Your life is a peaceful one, but I'm not sure it's a happy one.

Neither was he, not anymore. He'd believed it was, until recently. He liked his peace, his calm, his stability. But now it all felt lacking; a sense of discontent had been growing inside him since he'd let himself notice Gavin.

By Thursday afternoon, anxiety crept back in. When he got home, he took Chelsea to the park and played chase and fetch and Frisbee with her until they both collapsed on the grass panting. He couldn't be bothered to cook when they returned to the house, impulsively ordering take-out for the first time in years.

When he'd finished dinner, he attempted to sit down and work on his billing, but at the top of the pile were the notes from the last job he'd done for Gavin before their date. Sighing, he tore the page from his day planner and tossed it into the waste bin. He couldn't send Gavin a bill now, not after what had happened.

Unable to concentrate on anything else, he went down to the basement and lifted weights until he hit muscle failure. He lay there panting on the weight bench until his arms stopped trembling before dragging himself upstairs to the shower, pausing for a long moment to look thoughtfully at the kitchen phone.

I won't call him. I won't.

He couldn't put himself in a position to go through that again, to watch another person sicken and die, to lose….

… someone who mattered to him.

Friday morning, Devon called to cancel their plans to meet for beers. Hannah was ill with a nasty summer cold, and he decided to stay home to pamper her. Derrick wished Hannah a speedy recovery and hung up.

Shit. He leaned against the kitchen wall and let his head thud back against it. After several long, slow breaths, he collected himself and went about his day.

He spent the early evening fidgeting in front of the TV with Chelsea. He tried going to bed just after sunset, but he lay staring at the ceiling, unable to sleep. When he stopped himself from reaching for the bedside phone, he swore and dressed quickly, slamming out of the house to his truck.

I'm not going to see him.

He went east on I-696 from Ferndale, rather than continuing north to Royal Oak where Gavin lived. He took the highway to the far side of Detroit before heading south on I-94 toward Detroit itself. He opened the window to the muggy night air and turned up Skynyrd on the radio full blast. After a few minutes, he turned it off again. Instead of lifting his mood, the noise simply annoyed him.

It's not right. Wouldn't be fair to go to him. Not until you know whether you can take it, or not, if he turns out to be HIV positive.

West, then, on I-96, heading for I-275. He looked at the clock in his dash. *Besides, it's after eleven o'clock. It's too damn late to call or go see him.*

North along I-275 back toward I-696.

It's Friday, man. Who cares how late it is?

Could he do it? Could he take the risk of coming to care for someone whom he might have to watch die someday?

Assuming quite a bit there, aren't you? You don't know if you'll be with him in three weeks, much less three years, or thirty years.

East on I-696. The dash clock read eleven-thirty.

If you're gonna go, do it now.

His exit. Gavin's exit. South toward home, or north, to Gavin.

His heart beginning to race, he turned north.

He sat in the truck in the parking garage, staring at the clock.

11:45. You're already being rude, showing up this late. Go inside or leave.

He opened the door and stepped out of the truck, his palms sweating. On the elevator ride up, he drew slow, even breaths, trying to find his equilibrium.

He wondered if he looked anywhere near as panicky as he felt as he walked the few yards to Gavin's door. He wiped his palms on his jeans and made himself do it. The rap of his knuckles on the door sounded brutally loud in the silent corridor.

The door opened and Gavin stood there, pale and weary. Surprised. Confused. Wary. He smelled like cigarettes and beer.

They stared at each other as Derrick tried to find a way to breathe. His chest was too tight, the pounding of his own heart too loud, too fast.

He opened his mouth, his voice barely more than a raspy whisper.

"I'm sorry. Gav. I'm sorry. I'm sorry. Please...."

Gavin swallowed.

He deserved a damn good explanation, Derrick thought, frustration edging in on his nervousness. He deserved groveling and a long talk about what had happened and why.

But his words were gone, buried beneath a tide of *too much*. Too much feeling. Too much need. Too much remorse. Too much fear. His mouth worked uselessly, trying to force *something* out.

Too much. He couldn't. *He couldn't.*

Instead, he stepped forward and hooked a hand behind the back of Gavin's neck, drawing him into a desperate kiss, and prayed it would be enough for what words couldn't say.

CHAPTER TEN

HE DIDN'T KNOW HOW he ended up pressing Gavin back against the wall. It wasn't intentional. He half-expected Gavin to throw him out on his ass, but instead, Gavin just... Well, he wasn't sure what it was Gavin did, but when he took a step forward, Gavin's arms came around him, and then they were against the wall. Somewhere on the edge of his consciousness, the door slammed closed.

Gavin tasted just as good as he had before, *smelled* just as good. His body felt just as perfect. He buried his hands in Derrick's hair, his grip tightening, pulling, and that was perfect, too. Derrick pressed against him harder, moaning into his mouth.

The *wanting* was every bit as intense as it had been before; they both shook with it. Hard in their jeans, they moved together, seeking more contact. Hot, open, panting, his mouth met with Gavin's again and again. Polite decorum was discarded; they weren't tentatively feeling the way forward. He made no effort not to fuck Gavin's mouth with his tongue, and let Gavin fuck his in return.

Gavin shoved his hand into Derrick's back pocket and jerked him closer. Derrick shuddered, going still at the feel of Gavin's hand on his ass. He pulled his mouth away from Gavin's, his breath rapid. His hips, however, missed the memo that he was trying to slow down and continued to rock against Gavin.

He wanted Gavin. It was just that simple. Like a dam bursting, a flood of *need* surged through him. He was drowning and he knew it. He wanted to sink under and let the current take him, and at the same time push up to the surface, to catch his breath and escape the danger.

His hands shook as he held Gavin's waist.

"Are you all right?" Gavin murmured, and Derrick drew back to look at him. How could Gavin even ask him that, after what he'd done? Why had Gavin even let him—

He swallowed hard, nodding, looking at Gavin with concern. "I, um… I should be asking you that. I'm sorry, I shouldn't have just charged in like that. Without checking if you— I mean, I couldn't blame you if you didn't want this. If you'd rather we stop, or if you want me to leave, or if you wanna go someplace neutral to talk, I can do that. I don't wanna use *this* to make it all better. That's not what I'm here for."

Gavin looked stricken for a moment. And then he shook his head, closing his eyes. "No. Not yet. We'll talk later."

He wanted to accept that. He wanted to kiss Gavin again and forget all about the other shit, but the miasma of beer stopped him.

"How much have you had to drink?"

"I'm fine. I've only had a few, and most of those were a few hours ago."

Derrick drew a deep breath, nodding, and the shaking of his hands resumed as they moved up and down Gavin's waist unconsciously. "I'm not sure what… I mean, I don't… I've never…." He drew back to meet Gavin's gaze again, feeling the tension in his eyes and forehead. He wondered if he looked anywhere near as terrified as he felt.

"What do you *want?*" Gavin murmured, his lips brushing across Derrick's. His hand relaxed in Derrick's hair, stroking down to the back of his neck, soothing him.

His hands tightened on Gavin's waist, and he licked his lips, struggling to speak even those simple words. It had been so easy last weekend, when he hadn't had to say it, when it had just been Gavin's body straddling his, grinding down against him, moving toward exactly what he needed and couldn't find the words to request.

"This," he whispered at last. "This. Here. *You*. Please...."

The moment seemed to draw out forever, as they stood there with their foreheads touching, breathing together. Gavin's hand tightened in his back pocket. Gavin's open mouth slanted across Derrick's, his tongue sliding over Derrick's lips. Then *Derrick's* back was against the wall. Gavin pinned him, ground against him, as Gavin's knowledge took over where Derrick's desperation had begun.

Gavin jerked his t-shirt out of his jeans and shoved it up. Cool conditioned air brushed his skin, and Gavin's touch slid over his abdomen.

So long... so damn long.... It had been forever since he'd been touched that way. For that matter, he wasn't sure he'd *ever* been touched the way Gavin touched him, as though the feel of his skin was not only good, but *vital*. As though Gavin's fingers craved him. The sensitive skin of his stomach twitched, ticklish for a moment as his senses tried to remember what the hands of another person felt like.

"*Fuck*," Gavin whispered, pushing impatiently at Derrick's shirt. "Please. I want to touch you."

He drew back enough to tug his shirt over his head and let it fall to the floor. Gavin's hands swept over his skin, kneading his flesh as if he'd never felt another body before. He drew Gavin by the back of his neck into a rough, hungry kiss. It lasted only a moment, a violent clash of lips and tongues, and then Gavin pulled away and jerked his own shirt off, tossing it aside with a muffled clatter, his glasses trapped somewhere within its folds.

If Gavin's touch had been good, the press of his bare chest was even better. He could feel the race of Gavin's pulse under his thumb where it rested just under Gavin's jaw, telling him his need and fear and the inescapable sense of crossing the point of no return was shared. Gavin's grasp and gliding fingers were

113

everywhere; on Derrick's back, his shoulders, his ass. Groping, squeezing, kneading.

Gavin drew back enough to murmur against his mouth. "Come on." He took Derrick's hand and drew him down the hall to the first door. He kissed Derrick again, tender and cautious, and when he drew back, there was a silent question in his eyes.

"I want to do this. I want to feel this." His hand cupped the swell of Derrick's erection through his jeans. Derrick licked his lips and nodded. He pushed forward into Gavin's palm, watching Gavin's face. After a moment, his eyes drifted shut, accompanied by a moan, and Gavin urged him down onto the bed..

The bed. It was far easier to give himself over to the flow of kisses and touches than it was to sit there, understanding what he wanted, his determination edged with fear. Not of what they were about to do, but of what it might mean.

Still, he bent over and removed his work-boots and socks, pressing on. As Gavin approached, Derrick scooted back, taking a deep breath and reaching down to unbuckle his belt.

"Come on, leave something for me to do," Gavin scolded with a playful chuckle, pushing Derrick down and straddling him. Derrick moaned as Gavin deliberately moved. "I want to have some fun, too. It's like opening a present."

Derrick laughed, his head rolling back and his body jerking underneath Gavin's. Gavin gave him a delighted grin, the same one he used when Derrick reacted to his flirtations.

"That was… really cheesy."

Gavin chuckled. "Maybe, but it's also true." Before Derrick could decide whether or not to laugh at that, Gavin kissed him roughly. Derrick's hands explored his skin, the ridges of his ribs, the arch of his spine. When Gavin gripped his hair again, he lost all interest in banter.

He watched as Gavin drew away to dig in the drawer of the bedside table for a strip of condoms and a bottle of lube. Strangely, his nerves had abated. He felt calm, his fear receding as he blinked up at Gavin. Eager and accepting, he welcomed Gavin's weight back upon him when he'd tossed the condoms on the bed.

Gavin's hands and mouth began to move. His teeth nipped and scraped Derrick's neck. Derrick's fingers dug into the flesh of his shoulders, then slid up into Gavin's short hair. His restless fingers pressed against Gavin's scalp, massaging.

Gavin lay upon him, between Derrick's thighs instead of straddling him. That was even better. More of his weight covered Derrick's body; the pressure of their erections rubbing against each other increased.

And then Gavin moved lower, pausing to do things to Derrick's nipples that made him arch off the bed. Everywhere, Gavin's mouth and hands nipped and sucked, licked and stroked. He moved aside; his hand replaced his hips. It cupped and stroked through Derrick's jeans until Derrick was ready to beg him to just get on with it already.

He heard Gavin's breath hitch when he finally, *finally* opened Derrick's jeans and eased them down his hips with his underwear. Gavin's fingers ghosted along his dick, encircling it. He slid the foreskin up and over the ridge and traced it with an experimental fingertip. Derrick groaned, pushing up into that grasp, trying to take control of the surge of sensation that, coupled with the anticipation and the arousal, threatened humiliating consequences.

To both Derrick's relief and agonized disappointment, Gavin eased off almost before he'd begun. He grabbed a condom from the strip and tore the wrapper open, putting a little lube inside the tip before rolling it down Derrick's cock. Derrick didn't know whether or be grateful or crestfallen when the sensation of Gavin's stroking hand was muted to something manageable, but then it didn't matter because Gavin bent his head and took Derrick's dick into his mouth.

Oh, God!

He was pretty sure he shouted at the first onslaught, the moment the warmth of Gavin's mouth surrounded him. He pushed up, unable to control the eager thrust of his hips. Gavin withdrew a bit, pressing a restraining hand down on his stomach, and he gripped the comforter beneath him, holding it desperately as he fought to keep still.

Gavin's hand joined the effort, gripping the base of Derrick's cock as his mouth worked up and down the shaft. Derrick saw sparkles behind his eyelids. The scope of his awareness narrowed until all that remained were heat and suction and pressure. The strokes of Gavin's tongue worked their way around the head of his cock. Insensible words mingled with his gasps, but he had no idea which ones. He panted until he was dizzy with it, twisting his hands in the covers, wrestling against them as much as clinging to them.

The aching pressure grew tighter, heavier. He chased it and shrank from it in turns. He wanted the thunderous orgasm he knew was building and he wanted it never to end. Then it was upon him; it surged from his balls along his cock and wrenched a strangled shout from his throat. In its wake, it left him limp on the mattress, panting harshly.

"That," he breathed as Gavin stretched out above him, "was incredible. Thank you."

Gavin kissed his neck, laughing. "I don't know if you really ought to be thanking me for this, but you're welcome."

"Sorry, that was probably not the thing to say, was it?" He let his hands wander, over Gavin's shoulders and back, enjoying the feel of him too much to be all that self-conscious. "You feel good."

"So do you." Gavin's fingers combed through his chest hair, and Derrick's stomach twitched as they moved lower. He gave a quiet moan, his hands moving with more intent down Gavin's back. He paused at the waistband of Gavin's jeans, then licked his lips and cupped the tight, narrow swell of Gavin's ass.

No longer distracted by his own erection, he could feel just how hard Gavin was. Gavin closed his eyes and ground down against Derrick. His jeans clung to him, a little low on the hips, and Derrick squeezed, finding Gavin's ass firm.

Gavin moved above Derrick. "That feels good," he breathed, pushing his erection against Derrick's belly again. Derrick pulled him in harder, watching Gavin bite his lip as the pressure increased.

It was a moment longer before Gavin opened his eyes, murmuring, "Wait." Deftly, he slipped the condom off, knotted it, and dropped it in a wastebasket Derrick hadn't even noticed beside the bed. "There. Before we get too carried away."

"Oh. Right." Derrick colored, embarrassed that he'd forgotten.

Gavin looked pleased with himself as he lay down beside Derrick. Derrick rolled up onto his side and dipped his head to kiss Gavin, tentative as he tried to figure out what he would do next. Gavin responded by seizing his hair again. He transformed the kiss. It became hungry, demanding, and something within Derrick answered with determination. His arm curled around Gavin's waist; his hand slid over Gavin's ass, pulling him closer as Derrick's knee hooked forward between Gavin's legs.

Gavin groaned, riding Derrick's thigh, damn near humping it. His hands were everywhere. His tongue pushed into Derrick's mouth. Derrick met it with a curl of his own, sucking. Gavin rolled onto his back, giving Derrick access to his fly.

He inhaled a deep, slow breath, shoving nerves aside, and tugged Gavin's belt out of its buckle, reaching for the buttons.

Then Gavin's hand caught his, stopping him. Derrick looked up, taking his eyes off the actions of his hand to see Gavin watching him with a somber expression. "I don't want you to feel like you *have* to do this. Really. Just know that. Okay?"

"I know." Derrick nodded, meeting his gaze. "I want to."

He felt his face heating up again. He pulled his hand out of Gavin's and blatantly covered Gavin's cock with it. Gavin moaned as Derrick's thumb ran along the outline of his erection underneath the denim. He traced the ridge on either side of Gavin's fly, up and down, listening to Gavin's sounds, the hitches and gasps in his breath.

One by one, he opened the buttons down Gavin's fly, staring as the line of his cock was exposed. It strained against the stretchy burgundy cotton of his underwear. Derrick shoved his hand between Gavin's jeans and underwear, stroking along that bulge, and then inside the underwear themselves, gripping Gavin.

Impatiently, Gavin pushed his jeans and underwear down his hips, panting and gasping semi-coherent pleas. "Oh, God... oh, God, yes... just... just need..."

He replaced Gavin's hands with his own, tugging on his jeans and underwear. He didn't want to reveal just enough; he wanted Gavin bare, wanted all of him. His legs were as lean and muscled as his ass had been under Derrick's hands, but before Derrick could admire them for long, Gavin grabbed him behind the neck and jerked him down into a greedy kiss.

Derrick let himself be pulled down; he met Gavin's mouth with an eager clash. Gavin thrust his hand into Derrick's hair, gripping the back of his neck with the other, and Derrick found his own touch becoming unintentionally rougher. His fingernails scraped back up Gavin's thigh.

Dear God. The sound Gavin made, the way his body undulated, seeking more, was indescribable. He played with Gavin the way he'd learned to play with himself, to make what might have been just a perfunctory jerk-off something better. He watched Gavin's responses; his face looked nearly tormented, his hips rolled and shifted, wordlessly begging for more. Derrick's lips curved up a little in a tight, fierce smile, and he wrapped his hand around Gavin's dick.

Gavin went boneless, falling back against the bed, moaning. Derrick watched for a moment, his eyes moving from Gavin's enraptured face down his body to where his hand moved up and down Gavin's cock. It felt different without the slide of the foreskin he was accustomed to. Not bad, but strange, not to be able to glide up and down so easily. He stretched out, brushing the soft stubble on Gavin's chin with his lips in a half-kiss as Gavin's hips rose and fell to lend his own momentum to the strokes of Derrick's hand.

Gavin's cock felt warm, heavy, incredibly alive in his hand. Somehow stroking it felt much more *real*, much more *everything* than his own felt. He wondered just when that dry friction would become irritating, and decided not to test the limit. Gavin made a disappointed sound as Derrick released his dick and began searching in the tangled covers for the lube he'd seen Gavin toss aside.

"Um, wait. Here." Gavin opened his eyes and did his own digging, emerging with the bottle first and offering it to Derrick, his eyes glassy and eager.

"Thanks." He flipped open the cap and poured it into his palm before kissing Gavin. He took his time with that kiss, drawing it out rather than rushing. If it happened he never got this chance again, he thought, he wasn't going to hurry through it. He wrapped his hand around Gavin's cock again, slicking lube along it as he stroked down. Gavin's response was instant and breathtaking. He caught a handful of Derrick's hair and thrust up into Derrick's slick grip, sliding through his fist.

His strokes faltered, his concentration broken by the pull on his hair. He pressed Gavin down, and stretched out beside him, kissing and nipping his jaw. He stroked slowly, ignoring Gavin's impatient movements until he began groaning in frustration. Then his grip tightened; his hand curled around the head of Gavin's cock with a twisting motion on each pass. He lifted his head and looked down at the sight of Gavin's cock sliding through his hand. When he stopped moving for a moment, squeezing firmly, Gavin continued pumping, fucking Derrick's fist until Derrick took up the rhythm again, faster and harder than before.

Gavin clutched at his shoulders and back as Derrick bent his head to kiss the faint, soft hair on Gavin's chest. His palm returned

119

to the head, cupping it, squeezing, twisting just the slightest bit around the crown on the down-stroke. He pressed his lips to Gavin's shoulder, listening to his wordless sounds of desperation.

Gavin's gasps and groans grew hoarser, louder, his breath hitching and catching. His face was strained, his mouth open as he panted. "More… faster… oh, God, please…."

He tucked his face against Gavin's neck, his grip on Gavin's cock growing tighter, pumping faster. He murmured soft encouragements against the racing pulse along Gavin's neck, while Gavin's hips moved without cease, thrusting up to meet Derrick's strokes.

"Oh, God… just… oh, God, don't stop… oh, fuck yes…!"

When he lifted his head to kiss Gavin, he found himself caught by the back of the neck again. Gavin's hand tangled in his hair, and his mouth opened, gasping against Derrick's. His tongue thrust messily, without thought for decorum. Derrick returned the sloppy kisses, eager and unrestrained, feeling a surge of power and triumph at Gavin's urgency.

A little harder, a little faster, and Gavin's back arched. His dick throbbed in Derrick's hand, spurting across his stomach, before he sank back down onto the mattress. Gavin's hand released the grip on his hair it had never occurred to Derrick to mind.

Derrick released his grip on Gavin's cock and laid his head against Gavin's shoulder, listening to his ragged breathing. Now that he had nothing to do but think over what had happened, an unaccustomed doubt assailed him, only partially assuaged when Gavin's arms came around him. The embrace calmed him; it felt comforting and *right* in some way the rational part of his brain protested that it shouldn't be on so short an acquaintance.

Maybe it was just the feeling of being held by someone after so long.

"Was that all right?" he murmured as Gavin's breathing slowed, distracting himself from questions he couldn't hope to answer.

Gavin lifted his head and gave him an incredulous, amused look. "Oh, my God, yes. It was *better* than all right."

Derrick chuckled a bit self-consciously, blushing again as he laughed at himself for the ridiculous concern. But Gavin slid a hand alongside his face and drew him up for a kiss that was more tender than passionate. Derrick returned it, a bit of confused disquiet welling up within him. He knew what to do with the passion; he wasn't so sure about the tenderness. It implied things that had nothing to do with simple lust and everything to do with....

... stuff he had no business thinking at this point.

He pushed it aside and lifted his head with a crooked smile. Distraction. That was the key.

"Good. Want me to go get you a washcloth? Or anything?"

"If you don't mind." Gavin nodded, looking down the length of his torso with a wry smile, utterly unashamed.

After another kiss, he rose, pulling his pants back up and buttoning the top button. He debated for a moment whether to clean Gavin himself, or if that was too intrusive. Too intimate. Was not doing it impolite? Was he expected to leave now, or would Gavin want him to stay the night? What was the protocol? How did all this work?

Jesus, why didn't he know this sort of thing? His twenties suddenly seemed like a complete waste.

Was there a handbook he should pick up?

He decided to err on the side of under-assuming and handed Gavin the cloth.

He sat on the edge of the bed, frowning, opting for honesty. "I'm not sure what comes next, here. This isn't the sort of thing I usually—or ever—do."

"Um, well, I guess that depends on what you want." Gavin busied himself wiping his stomach, but Derrick could see him bite his lower lip. His tone was diffident, and he wouldn't meet Derrick's eyes. "We could kiss again. We could just lay here, hold

121

each other. We could say good night. We could do more. It's up to you."

All of those sounded like very good options, none of which answered the question he'd been trying to ask.

How *did* one phrase the question, *Is this a one-night stand or something else?*

"I'd say it's up to both of us. But just to clarify, you don't want me to leave?" He kept his voice quiet and steady, determined to accept any answer with equanimity.

"I'd prefer it if you didn't, actually," Gavin replied with a shake of his head.

He tried not to look as relieved as he felt, nodding calmly. "That's good. That's the first question answered. I didn't want to go, but I didn't want to," *look like I'm looking for more out of this than I have any business doing,* "assume anything."

He pushed his jeans off his hips, debating whether or not to keep his underwear. Then he laughed at himself; being shy seemed futile at this point. Something chimed behind him as he discarded those, too, and Gavin reached over the side of the bed for his own jeans and withdrew his phone from the pocket.

"Bad form, I know, but I've got to check this text here."

Derrick gave him space, wondering who would be texting after midnight on a Friday. It couldn't be business at this hour, could it?

Gavin sounded apologetic. "It's Andi. I never told her I was going out tonight, and she was expecting a call from me. She must be worried sick. I'll need to call her. Please, get comfortable."

Derrick lay down on his side, trying to look more casual than he felt, and nodded. "That's fine. Go ahead. I'll wait here."

He watched as Gavin disappeared down the hallway toward the living room and out to the balcony, then closed his eyes with a slow sigh once he was gone, trying to figure out what he should do next.

CHAPTER ELEVEN

HE WASN'T SURE WHAT TO DO WITH HIMSELF once Gavin left. Lying naked on the bed felt awkward and conspicuous in a way he hadn't felt in Gavin's presence.

Unable to lie still, he busied himself tidying the room. He peeled back the rumpled bedclothes and smoothed them, stopping just short of making the bed. He gathered his discarded clothes from the floor and laid them across the back of a chair, then checked the locks on the door Gavin had carelessly thrown closed earlier. Gavin's shirt and glasses were gone from the hallway floor.

Deciding he was thirsty, he walked naked to the kitchen, grabbing two empty beer bottles off the island and rinsing them in the sink along the way. Looking through the patio door at the balcony, he could see Gavin's back. He held his phone to his ear, and Derrick would see a wispy stream of smoke rising above his head. He filled two glasses with water and took them back to the bedroom before Gavin could turn around and see him standing there staring.

When Gavin returned, Derrick lay on his side in a strange compromise with modesty that probably only made sense in his own mind. Gavin ducked into the bathroom and emerged smelling like soap and toothpaste, reminding Derrick he hadn't brought a toothbrush.

"Sorry about that," he murmured as he undressed. He set his glasses and phone on the table next to the bed before slipping under the covers and stretching out beside Derrick.

Derrick lifted his head just enough to shake it, then lay down again. "It's fine. I'm just trying to figure things out."

Gavin propped himself up on his elbow. "Like what?"

"Well, I'm a guy who likes things simple, you see." Derrick shifted onto his back, staring up at the ceiling, his fingers fidgeting against his abdomen as he thought. "And the reason—well, one of the reasons—I gave up on the idea of dating was it's all really complicated. There's a ton of rules, none of which I know the first damn thing about, and to tell the truth, I never particularly cared to learn."

He sighed. "Like, just now. Here I am, laying in nothing but my skin, and I'm wondering, if I lay here exposed, am I shameless? If I get under the covers, am I presuming too much? You see?"

Gavin stared at Derrick a moment.

Then he burst into laughter. Which, Derrick supposed, was an appropriate reaction, considering how ridiculous he was being.

"You are over-thinking this *entirely* too much."

"Am I?" Derrick chuckled, closing his eyes for a moment in amused chagrin.

"You are. I didn't think you were shameless." Gavin sighed, still smiling. "I'm more inclined to appreciate the view than to worry about propriety."

Derrick laughed, tucking his head into the pillow to disguise a blush.

"Just do what feels *right*. If it doesn't feel right, you aren't going to enjoy yourself, and that's not worth any amount of your time."

Derrick lay there for a moment, quelling the urge to make an observation about the apparent contradiction between the philosophy Gavin had just espoused and what he had said the previous weekend about his relationship with his ex and doing things he hadn't wanted. It wasn't his place to say such a thing. He didn't know what had happened between them; he couldn't make any judgments.

"Yeah, that makes sense," he said, shifting to join Gavin under the covers. Gavin immediately curled against him. Derrick hesitated a moment. Alarm bells in his head went off, warning him of the dangers of being too intimate with anyone.

But they didn't stop him from wrapping his arm around Gavin, laying his cheek on top of Gavin's head.

Gavin felt good next to him, despite the danger.

"This works," he murmured with a sigh.

Gavin's body against his didn't quite feel relaxed, even when his arm draped across Derrick's waist so he could press closer. A tension hung between them, not quite uncomfortable, but expectant.

Then Gavin blew out a nervous breath. "I guess I should ask this, since I won't be able to relax until I do. Why did you leave?"

Derrick closed his eyes, stifling a soft groan. He'd dreaded the question since they'd stopped groping each other long enough to think rationally for two consecutive minutes. Looking at Gavin, touching him, his reasons for walking out no longer seemed satisfactory. Nor did they seem like anything Gavin needed to hear.

He didn't *need* to hear about the worst-case scenario, the one that terrified Derrick. He had no doubt Gavin thought about anything *but* as he waited and worried over what his future might be like, or even how much of a future he might have. He didn't need to hear how Derrick had taken Gavin's struggle and made it about his issues and fears.

He didn't need to think about the possibility that he might die.

Derrick swallowed, and his arms tightened around Gavin. "I... You need to understand, it wasn't about you. Not really. I wasn't worried for my safety or anything. That's just stupid and I know better than that."

"I know." He felt Gavin's hand moving up and down between his ribs and his waist in a light caress. "I just wondered. If you didn't want someone who was sick. If you didn't want to have to deal with that, um, hassle."

He was so close to the truth, but for all the wrong reasons. Derrick kissed Gavin's forehead, his reply little more than a murmur.

"If you mean using condoms and taking the meds you'd have to take and all that? No. That wasn't it. It was just...."

I was afraid of losing you. I was afraid of going through it all over again.

He stopped himself from blurting it out. Even if it hadn't implied feelings he had no business implying this early on, it would still be the wrong thing to say.

For the first time, he felt capable of confiding in someone how those last years with his grandparents had been. How they had left him exhausted and drained and despairing. How many nights he'd awoken hours before dawn wondering if he was even still alive anymore, wondering if he could make it through another week without breaking. How he'd kept it all to himself, because he had few people he *could* tell, and because he didn't want to burden those he did have. Miss Ingrid had intuited it, but she'd never pressed him to talk about it, and he wouldn't have been capable of doing so if she had. Gram had tried to ask, but he could tell her least of all how heavy a burden caring for her and Gramps by himself had become. He couldn't tell her how it was destroying him to see Gramps so lost and to see her in such pain. He couldn't tell her how empty he knew his life would be, once they were gone.

Finally, he could share all he'd kept to himself back then. But it wasn't right. It wasn't what Gavin should hear. He had his own fears and burdens, and Derrick wouldn't add to them.

"I'm sorry," he murmured. "It was a stupid, selfish thing I had no business worrying about when you're dealing with all this. I'm sorry."

Gavin's voice was soft. "I just worried. A lot. It ate at me."

"Worried?" Derrick huffed an incredulous laugh. "You'd be within your rights to be pissed off."

Gavin shrugged. "Maybe I was, for like, half a minute. But I have at least part of the blame there. I should have told you about it that night at the bar, before I ever let things get to the point they got to. I held back and I shouldn't have. That wasn't fair to you."

"Why did you?"

"I guess I was just enjoying it too much. I wanted to let myself have a little fun before I had to dump an ice-cold bucket of reality all over things." Gavin's mouth tightened. "But I wouldn't have pegged you for a guy who walks out."

"Yeah, well, if you'd asked me before that moment, I would have said I wasn't either. I'm sorry," Derrick whispered, drawing away a little as a tight, anxious feeling began to squeeze his chest. He stared up at the ceiling, seeking air and space without meaning to distance himself. "I'm sorry."

"I shouldn't have asked." Gavin's sigh sounded dissatisfied with the answer, and Derrick couldn't blame him.

He rolled back toward Gavin and tightened his arm around him again. "Yeah, you should have. You deserve at least that much."

A small shiver rippled through Gavin. "It's just that I'm scared. I'm *really* scared. I'm fucking *terrified*, if I'm going to be honest. And then the first time I try to be with someone else, and—and I was *honest* with you, and...."

Derrick winced at the hurt in Gavin's voice, and brought his other arm around him, embracing him fully. "I know. I—Jesus, I'm not sure how many times I can say I'm sorry before you get sick of it, but I'm willing to hit that limit. If you tell me what I can do to make this—not better, I know, but at least more bearable for you—I'll do it."

Gavin shifted, tucking himself against Derrick. "Talking helps. I think. I feel a little better, at least, than I did before you got here. Though I doubt this talk is what did it."

Derrick chuckled, grateful Gavin wasn't in a position to see his blush. "I'm willing to do more of *that*, too, if it'll help."

Gavin grinned back. "I'll take you up on that in the morning."

Drawing a deep breath, his tone muted, Derrick asked, "If I promise not to be an asshole this time, would you tell me what happened? I'd like to understand."

"You mean with Lukas. My ex." Gavin gnawed on his bottom lip, and in the dim light of the bedroom, Derrick could tell his fair skin had gone a bit paler, because his freckles seemed darker.

"Yeah." Derrick nodded, though second thoughts about asking began to assail him. "You don't have to talk about it. If you don't want to. Or can't. But if you can, I'd like to know."

Gavin took a shaky breath, and Derrick's stomach felt tense as he waited for Gavin to answer.

"It started off great," Gavin answered, his voice a murmur against Derrick's chest. "He made me feel wanted. And I liked that. And then he made up some bullshit excuse, said he was going to be out on his ass with nowhere to live, like three weeks after we started dating. I can see now he was after a meal ticket, but at the time... I couldn't let that happen, you know? It just wouldn't be right. So I had him move in.

"And then it all went bad. He'd argue against everything I said, and he would twist everything that came out of my mouth to make it *wrong*, or a slight against him. He never heard what I actually said. He just made things up and accused me of saying them." Gavin's voice got louder, his tone one of confused protest, his words coming faster, spilling out in a rush despite his initial reluctance, as though he'd been dying to say them. He was tense in Derrick's arms. "He would pout and give me the cold shoulder and play the martyr if I didn't give him what he wanted. And he would tell me the things I liked or things I did were *bad* and I should be *ashamed* of them."

Derrick swallowed, nodding. He quelled the urge to ask what sort of things Lukas had disapproved of. Perhaps it might give him a better idea of what had happened, but it might also seem like a prompt for salacious details.

Gavin provided them anyway.

"It wasn't just sex—though there were a lot of things there he didn't want me to do, things I liked, things I was *good* at—but just, like, *video games*. You know, it's not like I even do it that often. An hour here and there once or twice a week when I've got nothing better to do. But he *hated* it. Told me I should be doing 'more important' things without ever specifying what sort of 'more important' things I should be doing in the ten fucking minutes I was waiting for the pasta to boil."

Gavin raked a hand through his tousled hair. "I had to stop bringing my work home. He would never let me pay attention to it. He just didn't like my attention being on anything but him. Even when he ignored me to do his own thing, I couldn't let myself be distracted by anything but him. I think that's why he didn't like me spending time with Andi. At all. I don't think he was jealous of her. He didn't think I'd cheat on him with her. He just wanted me at his beck and call."

"Or he wanted to isolate you," Derrick murmured before he could stop himself. He hadn't meant to put his two cents in, but Gavin's words had struck a chord. Gavin looked at him and then he had no choice but to continue. He shrugged uncomfortably. "My friend's wife. She works for an organization that helps battered women. It's an abusive husband trick. Isolate his wife, or girlfriend, or whoever. Cut her off from the other people who care about her. Then there's no one to intervene. No one she can run to. No one to see her bruises."

Gavin stared at him wide-eyed, and Derrick grimaced, regretting his impulsive interruption. "Sorry. I shouldn't have... I mean, I'm not trying to imply you're like a battered wife. Ignore me. I really should keep my mouth shut."

Gavin shook his head, looking stunned. "No, I just didn't expect anyone to see it that way. Only Andi has ever called it," he swallowed. "Abuse. You're right. There was never any physical abuse, of course, but—"

Gavin fell silent, letting his head rest on Derrick's chest again.

"At first, he helped keep the apartment clean, but then somehow I was coming home in the evening and everything was a mess. And when I asked him what he'd done all day, he got defensive and said he'd been very busy working and I couldn't expect him to interrupt himself. So I was paying all the bills and cleaning his mess and my own. And it's not like I couldn't afford it, but I don't think I'm unreasonable for feeling used. But when I complained, he suggested I hire someone to clean the apartment if I didn't like it, since I could afford it. Like it was no big deal."

Gavin sighed, pausing for a moment. When he spoke next, his voice was scarcely a murmur, low and—to Derrick's ears—ashamed.

"You know how I said I didn't *want* to not be using protection with him? The first time we didn't, he'd gotten me drunk. *Really* drunk. And, well, after that it was all the guilt trips, the 'don't you trust me?' And then it was 'but you did it before' and 'don't be such a fucking pussy' and the *worst* times when he just… went into a rage when I brought it up and yelled that I should just shut up and do it anyway and stop *nagging* him about it."

"Shit," Derrick whispered, swallowing hard. He fought to keep from blurting out the thought, the word, which came to mind. He felt adrenaline surging through him, making his heart race and his chest tight as anger took hold. His eyes narrowed, hard and flinty.

The heavy note of shame in Gavin's voice persisted as he continued. "I told him to get out when, um… You know, he doesn't think HIV is dangerous? That's what it all came down to. Have you heard of that? I looked into it after I threw him out. It's a whole fucking movement of people who think that HIV is harmless, and that antiretrovirals are what kill you. Apparently it's all a big *conspiracy*," Gavin sneered, his voice becoming more

130

animated. "Researchers don't want to admit to it, because their funding would dry up, and Big Pharma doesn't want to admit to it because they make too much money off the 'AIDS myth' and the government doesn't want to admit to it because they engineered the whole thing to exterminate minorities and gays. Can you fucking *believe* that?"

Derrick blinked, disbelief pushing aside the surge of seething anger. "You're serious?"

Gavin nodded. "Once he told me, that's when I ended it."

Derrick rubbed his head, troubled and filled with sorrow for what had been done to Gavin, and deeply concerned. "Jesus. Person like that would be a ticking bomb. And he never told you he hadn't been tested?"

"No, he didn't." Gavin sighed with a resigned shake of his head. "The only time it really came up was the night I was drunk. And he assured me it'd be fine, and I was so fucking plastered that…."

Gavin shrugged helplessly, his words tapering off. Derrick stared at the dimly lit ceiling, grimacing as he struggled with whether or not to ask the question echoing inside his mind.

"What is it?" Gavin asked, sounding far too cautious for Derrick's comfort.

"I don't—" Derrick rubbed his forehead, starting over. "I'm trying to figure out how to not make this sound judgmental. I'm not judging. I'm not criticizing, and I'm sure as hell not trying to make you feel like you're to blame for what happened. I just want to understand, you know?" He didn't know if it was possible, really, to understand. The situation was as incomprehensible to him as it was tragic for Gavin. But he asked anyway. "Why did you let him do that? Treat you that way, I mean? Why didn't you tell him to get the fuck out sooner?"

Gavin's lips tightened, and he drew a deep breath before answering. "It was a gradual thing. Before I knew it, I could hardly do a thing without him throwing a fit. When I tried to negotiate

131

and settle things, he kept escalating them. I was always walking on eggshells when he'd lock himself in the room."

"The room? You mean the office?" Another piece of the puzzle fell into place.

Gavin nodded. "It was his studio. If I made a noise, even while I was trying to clean up *his* mess, I was disturbing him."

"Disturbing him doing what?"

"His *art*," Gavin sneered again, a soft snort punctuating his words. "His art that he claimed everyone loves, and yet nobody ever buys it."

Derrick gave a wry smile, kissing the top of Gavin's head, and murmured, "Ah, well. That explains that."

"Explains what?" Gavin asked, tilting his head back.

"That painting, or whatever it is, hanging on the wall in your living room. It doesn't—" *Look like anything resembling art?* "—suit you. He painted it, didn't he?"

Gavin groaned. "Oh, God. I forgot about that."

Derrick shrugged. "Sorry, that's beside the point. It just suddenly made sense to me why you have it. I didn't mean to interrupt."

Gavin shook his head. "No, no. I just—ugh. I forgot I still had that up there. Yeah, he painted it. It was supposed to be a statement about his *cause*."

Derrick lifted an eyebrow as Gavin snorted. "His cause is the stomach flu?"

Gavin's shoulders jerked and his lips clamped down, his eyes crinkling as he restrained a smile. "No. It's his fucked-up version of 'AIDS awareness.'"

"Oh. Riiight." Derrick fought a smile of his own, shaking his head.

Gavin fell silent for a long moment, the fleeting amusement fading from his face. "When he left, when I confronted him about what he might have done to me, he told me that nobody else would want me now, except him."

Derrick's chest ached. He cupped Gavin's jaw, turning his face up.

"It's not true."

"I know that, deep down inside. I know that. But when you walked out the door, it *felt* true."

Derrick's throat tightened, and he swallowed against the knot, stroking his thumb across Gavin's lips.

"I'm sorry," he whispered. "I didn't know. I'm sorry."

"You couldn't have known," Gavin murmured with a shake of his head, pressing a soft kiss to Derrick's thumb.

"I swear, it was never about you. At least not in that way." Now, more than ever, it seemed ridiculous that he'd been so worried about his own emotional well-being after what Gavin had struggled with. "It was selfish. Completely selfish. And not even a bit rational. I panicked, okay? I got scared, and I panicked. Not, you know, not about my safety. It was—" He shrugged, unable to find any better way of describing it. "—Other stuff. History. Baggage. Stuff that shouldn't matter."

Gavin fell silent a long moment. Then he nodded. "Okay."

"I'm sorry. You deserve an answer, and I wish I had a better one to give you."

"I understand."

Derrick laid his cheek against Gavin's hair. "Thank you."

Gavin lifted his head to give him a quizzical look. "You're welcome?"

"Not just for understanding. But for, well, letting me in the door's a good place to start."

Gavin smiled, and Derrick felt his chest tighten. "If I remember correctly, I only had the door open. *You* stepped inside."

"Well, you didn't throw me out on my ass. That helped."

"I don't know if I could, even if I'd wanted to. And you did a pretty good job of making sure I didn't want to." Gavin's voice dropped to a low, sexy note.

Derrick pressed an obliging kiss to his lips, blushing. Not so much at Gavin's tone as at his own all-too-eager response. He hadn't popped wood this often in someone's presence since he was a teenager. But Gavin's eyes were taking on a heavy-lidded look that made him constrain the impulse. "I would've gone if you'd told me to. I'm glad you didn't."

"Do you know how many times I pulled your name up in my phone over the last week?" No longer flirting, Gavin pulled back to meet Derrick's eyes, his face open and honest, something raw and vulnerable about the edges. Derrick felt the tightness in his chest redouble. A sudden surge of fear welled up inside him.

"Probably—" He drew a deep breath, admitting, "Probably about as many times as I had to talk myself out of calling, or coming over." He closed his eyes, hoping Gavin wouldn't see his fear, and kissed him again.

It took a while, for Gavin to settle back down against his chest.

"What are your plans for the weekend?"

"I'll have to leave in the morning, to go feed Chelsea and for a change of clothes. Usually Saturday is our day to go to the park. Wanna come? I could make us breakfast, you could meet Chelsea, hang out at the park with us. If you don't have plans."

"Nah, usually Saturday morning, it's me and the Xbox. Or me and my work, if I have any." Derrick yawned reflexively as he saw Gavin cover a yawn with his hand. Maybe sleep had been hard to come by for both of them, the past week. Or, he thought with a wry smile, it was just post-orgasmic endorphins dragging them under. "I do have plans with Andi tomorrow evening, though."

Derrick smiled. "Okay. Devon and I tentatively rescheduled our usual Friday night plans, so I might be busy too. I wasn't sure about Saturdays because I don't know much about your family. Wasn't sure if you had dinner with your mom or went to synagogue or anything."

Gavin's eyes widened a little, and he smiled, looking amused. "Oh, *wow*. You really don't miss a detail, do you?"

"My friend's wife is Jewish, so I recognized your mezuzah."

"I generally go on Friday night, so that's not really something to worry about this weekend."

"Okay, that's good to know. It'll save me asking you out on any Friday dates. I guess the only other question is, do you have a spare toothbrush I can borrow?"

Why was that so hard to ask? he wondered, forcing the question out. Maybe because it made the fact that he would be staying more real?

"I'm pretty sure I have an extra, sure." He could hear Gavin's voice becoming drowsy. "Want me to go look now?"

"Not just yet." Derrick kept his arm around Gavin, refusing to move. Lying there, Gavin tucked against him, was too nice. Comfortable. Secure. *Not alone.*

He hated the voice of fear inside him that cautioned against becoming too reliant on the feeling.

"I just didn't plan this. It wasn't something I prepared for."

"Yeah, neither had I," Gavin mumbled. "I honestly thought I was just going to have a beer with some co-workers, come home, and watch TV until I fell asleep."

"I was just out for a drive," Derrick admitted. "I'm glad I didn't stop myself from coming."

Gavin's arms tightened around him, and his voice slurred, almost inaudible.

"Me, too."

A few seconds later, he heard Gavin's breathing take on the deep, steady rhythm of sleep. He lay still for some time listening to it, determined not to wake Gavin by moving too soon. Only when he was in danger of falling asleep as well did Derrick ease himself out of Gavin's arms and slide out of the bed.

He covered Gavin with the blankets, looking down at him a long moment. A strange, protective feeling scratched at the back of his mind as he replayed their conversation. Shaking it off, he headed into the bathroom. A quiet hunt through the cabinets unearthed a wrapped toothbrush with a dentist's logo on the handle. Hoping he wasn't misstepping, Derrick helped himself to it.

When he returned to the bed, Gavin had sprawled out a bit. Smiling at the sight, Derrick tucked himself in wherever he could find room, moving as close as he dared without waking Gavin. He was still smiling when he fell asleep.

CHAPTER TWELVE

ALL THE WALLS OF GAVIN'S BEDROOM WERE INTERIOR, so Derrick awoke with no sense of time, except for a hint of sunlight reaching down the hallway from the great room to lighten the crack under the bedroom door. He fumbled at the bedside table where he'd seen Gavin drop his phone and thumbed the touchscreen, smiling to himself to realize just how late he'd slept.

"You okay?" Gavin mumbled sleepily.

He shook off the disorientation of waking somewhere strange, he laid the phone aside and settled back in as Gavin pressed up against him.

"Yeah. Just not used to sleeping this late."

"Oh God, you're an early bird," Gavin groaned, a chuckle bouncing through the sound. "That's it. Out. This'll never work."

Derrick laughed, rolling toward Gavin. "Oh, really? Because what I'm feeling against my hip seems to think otherwise."

"Hm, well, yes, there is that." Gavin pressed a kiss to his shoulder. "How would you feel if I said I don't want to get out of bed?"

His own morning wood registered a definite affirmative to that notion. "I doubt Chelsea will starve if I'm a little bit later getting home. I'll need to eat breakfast soon, but not just yet."

"Good. Because, actually—" Gavin's hand slid down his chest. "—I'm curious."

"Oh?" Derrick asked with a faint smile. He dropped his voice to what he hoped was a sexy murmur. "About what?"

"This," Gavin murmured as his hand covered Derrick's cock.

"Well," he cleared his throat, trying to sound more sophisticated and nonchalant than he felt. "You can't tell me you've never seen one before, so why—?"

"I've only ever been with one other guy who was intact, and he wouldn't let me explore. Said he didn't appreciate being treated like a curiosity."

"Ah." Derrick nodded, frowning as he remembered what Gavin had told him the night before. "Is that a thing? Is being curious bad? Because I'm not seeing why."

Gavin shrugged. "Personally, I don't think so. If I've connected the dots in what you've told me properly, you've never actually been with a man before me, right?"

"Mmhm." Derrick nodded, struggling to track the conversation. "Then there's the fact that the last time I had sex, I was barely more than a teenager. Tab A, slot B. We weren't that inventive, you know? I like to think what I lack in experience I'll make up for in enthusiasm."

Gavin laughed. "Yeah, I can feel your *enthusiasm*. But I imagine you're going to have some questions."

"Probably." Derrick chuckled, a sigh trickling through the sound. "Though right now your hand on my junk is making it hard to come up with any."

Gavin grinned. "Take your time."

Then Gavin's fingers crossed the twitchy, sensitive skin of his groin, and Derrick groaned.

"So?" Gavin prompted. Derrick opened his eyes to see Gavin biting his lip in concentration. "What do *you* like? I don't want to do anything you wouldn't enjoy."

"Well," he breathed, finding words a lot more difficult to string together. "It's, um, it's sensitive. *Really* sensitive." He held Gavin's hand and guided it along his dick, not attempting to wrap Gavin's fingers around it or roll the foreskin forward over the ridge. "Just do what you said you wanted to do. Explore. I'll tell you if something isn't working. Or if it is, for that matter."

Gavin looked a little bit uncertain, but he grasped Derrick's cock anyway, stroking with caution. The first time the foreskin slipped over the crown, Derrick's hips came up, moving just the smallest bit to meet the stroke. He moaned, his eyes closing.

Whoever had refused Gavin permission to do this was a grade-A moron, he decided, licking his lips. He let his hand fall to the pillow next to his head, making it clear he was open to and comfortable with whatever Gavin chose to do.

It didn't take long for Gavin to get the hang of it. Derrick gave himself over with soft moans and gasped encouragement, panting when particularly intense strokes made him catch his breath. He let his eyes fall shut again, sinking back into the sensations, relaxed and not the least bit self-conscious.

"That's really nice. God…."

Something brightened Gavin's voice a little; an audible smile, and Derrick felt his own lips curving in response.

"You like that? It feels good?" The pace of Gavin's stroking picked up.

"Mmhmm. It really does."

Then Gavin's other hand came into play, slipping between Derrick's thighs to fondle his balls, and the strokes up and down his dick got firmer, faster, more intense. Derrick fought to rein in his reactions, reluctant to let himself be pushed to the edge too soon. It was just too damn good, all the sensation with none of the effort to make it happen.

"Jesus… Gav…." he half-whispered, hardly aware he'd spoken as he concentrated on keeping his responses in check, still moving to meet Gavin's strokes.

Gavin's rhythm faltered for an instant before resuming.

"I like it when you call me that."

"Huh?" Derrick's eyes opened, looking up in confusion for a moment before he remembered what he'd said. "Oh." He moaned, closing his eyes again on the next wave of sensation, mustering a goofy smile. "Keep doing that, I'll call you anything you want."

139

"I'll keep that in mind." Gavin laughed, and Derrick smiled a bit broader in return. Somehow the laughter made it easier to hold on to control, and also made the entire experience more intense. Not just pleasurable, but *fun* in a way he wasn't sure he'd ever known sex could be.

Gavin experimented, altering his grip and tempo at intervals, beginning to linger longer and longer when he found something that dragged the most energetic reactions from Derrick. Derrick gave up on holding back, letting the feeling take him, his groans louder and more uncontrollable, begging between gasps.

"Keep… keep going… oh, God, please…."

He heard Gavin mutter something in response, encouragement, perhaps, and then the building orgasm broke over him with a shout and an almost painful tightening of his balls just before the first hard pulse of his cock.

He heard Gavin sigh as the pressure of his hand disappeared from Derrick's too-sensitive dick. "God, that's gorgeous."

Derrick mustered a short, breathless huff of laughter, too dazed even to blush. Gavin rose to retrieve a warm cloth for him, solicitously wiping the sweat from his face and chest before attending to the mess on his stomach. He pushed away the feeling of embarrassment that he hadn't tended to Gavin last night, and instead focused on the giddy feeling glowing inside him. He felt lighter than he had in years, so blissed-out and overjoyed he wanted to burst into laughter for no reason other than he felt *good*. He could feel an idiotic grin stretching across his face.

Post-orgasmic lassitude was nowhere to be found, this early in the morning. His ebullient mood asserted itself as he rolled, pushing Gavin onto his back and stretching out above him. He smiled, dropping a kiss to the underside of Gavin's jaw, moving down his neck. Gavin's dick was hard between their bodies, and Gavin pushed up against him needfully.

And then he froze up, burying his face against Gavin's throat. A spasm of uncertainty tried to choke his high spirits. His assertiveness faltered as quickly as it had come, leaving Derrick vulnerable and unsure.

Such a stupid, juvenile thing, to worry he wouldn't be a good lover. But ten years of abstinence following a rather infrequent and unremarkable post-adolescent sex life left him feeling like he was behind the sexual learning curve. Especially contrasted to Gavin's confidence.

"What is it?" Gavin's hands stroked his shoulders as Derrick hesitated.

"Teach me." Derrick whispered without any forethought or consideration, his heart hammering in his chest. "I want to know what you like, what you want. Help me learn you."

Gavin's hands stilled for a moment, his voice warm with understanding when he murmured back, "Gladly."

He let himself take comfort in Gavin for a moment, in the soothing caress of his hands, before he gathered up his nerve and moved down. Gavin groaned, and his hips lifted against Derrick's belly as Derrick's lips made their way to his nipple.

"God, yes," he breathed when Derrick's tongue flicked against his nipple. "Pinch the other one... yeah, like that... Harder. I like it when it hurts a little."

Oh, god.... Derrick moaned. Something in him melted when Gavin's hand brushed back his hair from where it had fallen forward around his face, sliding along his scalp. If he hadn't come so recently, he would have started to get hard again.

Gavin groaned when Derrick grasped his nipple, pinching. "Like that. Yeah...."

Gavin's body moved beneath Derrick's weight. His hand tightened in Derrick's hair, and that was good. So damn good.

Releasing Gavin's nipple, he began to move downward again. The closer he got to Gavin's groin, the better he smelled. Musk mingled with the remnants of whatever body wash or cologne Gavin used to create a scent that made Derrick want to bury his nose against Gavin's skin and just *inhale*.

When Gavin's hand relaxed in his hair, he realized he'd done just that.

He lifted his head, blinking in confusion as Gavin's hand drew back. "What is it?"

"I just don't want you to feel like I'm pushing you."

Derrick smiled, dropping a kiss on Gavin's hip, then reached for the strip of condoms on the bedside table, tearing one off. "I don't. It felt good."

"What, this?" Gavin's hand slipped back into his hair, fisting around it near the scalp. Another surge of arousal swept through Derrick, riding the breathless edge of danger mingled with arousal. His eyes snapped shut and his mouth fell open as Gavin pulled his head back. It felt like his bones had turned to gelatin, like he'd lost all volition, like he'd do anything, *anything,* that hand demanded of him.

It was both terrifying and sublime. Derrick's Adam's apple bobbed as it occurred to him that he wouldn't mind if Gavin *did* push him.

"That's *very* good to know," Gavin murmured, his grip relaxing once more. He looked both satisfied and predatory as Derrick opened his eyes again. "Keep going."

Derrick's hands weren't quite at their steady best as he tore open the wrapper and put a drop of lube in the condom before rolling it along Gavin's dick. He ignored the horrid scent and taste of latex and slid his mouth down Gavin's cock.

He discovered that giving a blow job was trickier than it seemed, watching it in porn. He couldn't seem to find a pace that evoked much of a reaction from Gavin, who stroked his hair patiently. He made encouraging sounds, but they weren't the desperate, pleasured noises Derrick hoped to hear.

After Gavin let him fumble for a few minutes, experimenting, he said softly, "Use your tongue."

As it had when Gavin's hand clenched in his hair, Gavin's words did something to Derrick, something that felt both safe and exciting. Not just the words. His voice. Derrick felt like he could do anything as long as that voice kept murmuring quiet demands. He faltered, trying to work out the best way to use his tongue as he moved, and he knew he'd found the trick when Gavin groaned.

"Yeah. God. Like that." Gavin shuddered, his body twitching as Derrick's tongue hit a sensitive spot on the next pass. "Just like that. Now... suck it."

He moaned around Gavin's cock without meaning to. That crude, clichéd, *filthy* demand used in a hundred bad skin flicks struck something inside Derrick, something that *wanted* instruction, *wanted* to obey. He gripped the base of the condom and sucked firmly.

Gavin grew louder, and Derrick sucked harder. His tongue stroked the ridge as he worked his way up to the head of Gavin's cock again. Gavin's hips came off the bed in short, jerky pushes, and his hand tightened in Derrick's hair again.

"God. Oh, yeah. Good... Oh, that's good. Now... all of that together...."

His groan vibrated along Gavin's cock, and he doubled his efforts, giving himself over to the rhythm. The hand in his hair seemed even more dangerous now. Gavin made no effort to push or control his head, but the implication was there. The thought that he *might* take control kept Derrick hovering between worry and yearning.

He pushed himself harder. The blossoming ache in his jaw and crick in his neck didn't matter. He drove himself on, ignoring them. What mattered were Gavin's urgent gasps and moans. Those were the sounds he wanted.

Gavin cried out, and beneath his tongue, Derrick *felt* the surge along the back side of Gavin's cock, the instant before he came. His hand twisted in Derrick's hair, his hips bucked, and then he collapsed back down on the bed, panting and shuddering with each after-pulse.

Trying to catch his own breath, Derrick laid his head on Gavin's thigh, pressing a kiss to the sweat-damp skin. When Gavin's panting slowed, Derrick discarded the condom and crawled back up the bed.

Gavin drew him down against his chest, in a reversal of their positions last night. He laid a hand on Derrick's head and tucked it beneath his chin, kissing Derrick's hair.

It felt good to be held. Safe. New and strange. He curled against Gavin and made himself stop over-thinking the tingle of vulnerability that shivered through him.

"Rest a few," Gavin murmured, chuckling. "*Enthusiasm*, indeed."

"Thanks." Derrick smiled, blushing, and pressed a kiss to Gavin's chest. He wanted to lay there all morning, but as he relaxed, a familiar, unsteady feeling began, trembling almost imperceptibly in his chest. He lifted his hand and found it shaking slightly. Reluctantly, he lifted his head. "Um, I really need to eat something."

Gavin frowned. "You okay?"

"Yeah, I just can't go too long without eating. Preferably something with some protein. Maybe we should get going so I can get to my place and make us breakfast. Or I guess it'll be more like brunch, won't it?"

"I guess it will." Gavin smiled, unwrapping his arms from around Derrick and sitting up. "Why don't you go ahead and get dressed, brush your teeth and whatnot, and I'll see what I can scare up to tide you over?"

When he came out of the bathroom, Gavin was out on the patio, smoking and talking on his cell phone. On the breakfast bar was a cup of yogurt and a toasted bagel slathered thickly with cream cheese, as well as a glass of orange juice. When Gavin came back in, he gave the kitchen a wide berth on his way toward the bathroom.

"You don't need to do that, you know," Derrick said, swallowing a bite of bagel. "Rush off, I mean."

"I'd still rather you like the way I smell."

Derrick shrugged. "Whatever you feel comfortable with, then."

Gavin disappeared down the hall to wash his hands and brush his teeth, then returned to the kitchen, leaning against the breakfast bar.

"Are you feeling better?"

"Yeah." Derrick nodded, dropping the empty yogurt container in the trash, and returned to the breakfast bar to finish his bagel. "Thank you."

"You're welcome. I don't tend to be a big breakfast person. This was all I had. Sorry it isn't much."

Derrick shook his head. "Don't worry about it."

"You're diabetic?"

"Hypoglycemic. If you ever see my hands shaking or I'm pale and sweating, or acting a little spacey or disoriented, feeding me is a pretty good bet. I might even get irritable or argumentative. Don't take it personally, okay?"

"Okay." Gavin pursed his lips thoughtfully. "How do you cope with that?"

"Mostly by keeping to a really strict schedule built around frequent meals." Derrick gave a self-effacing chuckle, wiping up his crumbs and loading his plate in the dishwasher. "I may be a bit of an unimaginative stick-in-the-mud, but I have my reasons for being so set in my ways."

"I don't know, I willing to bet you're *plenty* imaginative." Gavin gave him a wicked grin and Derrick flushed. "You need to hurry home to feed Chelsea?"

"Pretty soon, though I don't have to rush out the door just this instant. Chelsea has a dog door, so I don't have to let her out or anything. Mostly I think she's going to be really confused. I've never spent the night away before."

145

"Oh." For an instant, Gavin's face looked a little pitying, and Derrick realized how pathetic it must sound to someone else. It had never felt that way, as he'd gone about his life. He just hadn't had any reason to go anywhere.

He shrugged it off. "My job's low-stress, so I don't feel the need to take many vacations."

Gavin nodded and grinned again. "Well, if you don't need to get home immediately, maybe I can interest you in taking a shower with me?"

Derrick straightened from putting his empty glass in the dishwasher, smiling. "Now that sounds like a great idea."

"Good." Gavin caught Derrick with an arm around his waist and drew him close, backing him against the breakfast bar and kissing him firmly for the first time since they'd woken. The effect was immediate. Everything in Derrick, with the notable exception of a single body part, went warm and soft, melting. His hands itched to be on Gavin again.

"Good morning." Gavin looked ridiculously pleased with himself when he drew back and Derrick felt his own mouth curving in what he suspected was a rather goofy smile.

"Morning."

Best I've had in years, Derrick thought as Gavin led him to the shower.

He wondered how long it would be before it stopped feeling this way.

CHAPTER THIRTEEN

I<small>F</small> D<small>ERRICK HAD THOUGHT</small> his distraction after his date with Gavin the week before had been worthy of teasing from Devon, it was nothing compared to the *I just got laid* satisfaction oozing from his pores when he met Devon for pool Saturday night. The situation wasn't helped by the memories of the shower and Gavin's tongue on his ass he kept flashing back to every time he tried to focus in on the conversation. Strangely, though, Devon asked him no questions. He just gave Derrick a ridiculously pleased smile and said the first pitcher was on him.

When he called Gavin from bed that night, groggy and relaxed with too little sleep and too much beer, it was all he could do not to ask Gavin over for another round.

"I kinda wish I'd asked you to come back over tonight," Gavin murmured.

"I was just thinking the same thing."

"Okay, so if we both want this, and we agreed we'd just do what feels right, why didn't either of us say anything earlier?"

Derrick shrugged, smiling wryly. "Hell if I know. We're probably trying to play it cool, not seem too needy or something stupid like that."

Gavin snorted. "Screw needy. I'm horny. What are you doing tomorrow?"

When he'd stopped laughing and caught his breath, Derrick answered, "I have church in the morning, and then I take my elderly neighbor to the supermarket in the afternoon. After that I'm free, though."

"Come over for dinner?"

"I'd like that."

"Good. Bring an overnight bag? Or do you have a no sleepovers rule on work-nights?"

"Last I checked, I didn't have any rules at all for this sort of thing. I think I can handle being short of sleep Monday if you can."

He could almost hear Gavin's cheeky grin over the phone. "Count on it."

Miss Ingrid, with her usual sharp insight, began smiling before they were halfway to the market, managing to skirt just around the edges of being truly smug.

"You seem to be in better spirits," she remarked breezily, looking out the window rather than scrutinizing him.

Jesus, he really was wearing a *just got laid* sign around his neck, wasn't he?

Derrick allowed himself a slight lift of his lips and a noncommittal nod. "Thank you, ma'am. I am."

After a moment of silence, he saw her glance in his direction with eyes narrowed in mock annoyance.

"Are you really planning to torture a bored old woman with her own curiosity?"

Derrick's lips twitched before his face went innocent and blank. "'Course not, ma'am. I'd never treat a nice elderly lady in such a way," he protested.

She chuckled. "Of course. An interfering old biddy, however, is another matter, I'm sure."

"I would never call a nice elderly lady that, either."

He lost his battle with the urge to smile when she laughed aloud.

"Well, I hope you're happy with your young man."

Derrick shook his head. "His name's Gavin. And he's not— We're not— It's a good time. I mean, maybe someday, but not anything more just now."

"Then enjoy your good time," she murmured, patting his knee as he parked his truck outside the supermarket.

He spent the rest of the afternoon with Chelsea, offering her plenty of face-time and reassurance. Her sad eyes as Derrick packed his overnight bag, however, made him promise that he'd spend the next night at home with her, with or without Gavin.

When he got to Gavin's, he found Gavin had brought home sushi takeout for dinner.

Derrick eyed it skeptically.

"Don't like sushi?" Gavin asked with a raised eyebrow.

"Never tried it," Derrick murmured, setting down his bag, trying to push all the unappetizing descriptions he'd heard about sushi from his mind. "It's a bit outside my usual. I mean, come on. My mom's family was from the South, Gramps' parents came here from England just before he was born and Gram's parents were the descendants of German immigrants from up near Frankenmuth. I can't help but be a meat and potatoes guy." He grinned. "Bratwurst is about as exotic as I tend to get."

"I can make something else, if you'd like."

Derrick shook his head, sitting down at the table. "Nope. Can't say I don't like it until I try it, can I?"

To his pleased surprise, the sushi was quite tasty. He doubted it would ever feel truly filling to him, since his preference tended toward heavier food, but he enjoyed the flavor. After dinner, he busied himself cleaning the kitchen while Gavin stepped out on the balcony to smoke.

Unlike last time, he knew he wouldn't be running out, or asked to leave. He knew without a doubt where matters would head soon. The knowledge left his heart racing and his hands shaky. Friday night, he hadn't planned for it, hadn't anticipated it. He'd just plunged in and it had happened.

149

This was different. Nerve wracking and wonderful at the same time. When Gavin came back inside and completed his ritual of washing his hands and brushing his teeth, they would go to bed together. With each moment that ticked away, Derrick's sense of nervous anticipation increased, driving him steadily crazy. It wasn't like him, to *need* something this much. He wondered if he'd released something that couldn't be easily contained again—if ever.

He dried his hands on a dish towel and hung it on a hook as Gavin came in from the balcony and disappeared into the bathroom. He returned and leaned against the island counter, smiling. "Thank you, by the way."

"For what?" Derrick asked, glancing around the kitchen to see if any dirty dishes or smudges still lurked before he called the job done.

"For taking care of the dishes. I appreciate it."

"Least I could do, after you had me over to dinner." Derrick shrugged, leaning against the counter opposite Gavin. His mouth twitched as he took in their positioning. What had been so easy to banter about last night on the phone felt different now, face to face. The air was thick with expectation; his skin tingled in anticipation of the first touch.

He licked his bottom lip, staring at Gavin. He should just close the distance and be done with it, but he couldn't quite seem to push aside his nerves enough to make himself do it. It was more now. In ways he couldn't possibly hope to understand, whatever was happening here between them was more. And it terrified him just how much he wanted it. To move forward, to follow where this would lead, to *live* again.

But doing so meant leaving behind everything that was comfortable and safe.

Was it experience, or just greater courage that made Gavin make the first move instead? Gavin reached out to run a finger down the front of Derrick's shirt from the notch in his collarbone to the bottom of his sternum.

"I think your company was repayment enough, but all right, then. I can accept help with the chores."

"Good." Derrick gave a self-conscious laugh. "It's goofy but I kinda like cleaning."

Gavin's smile broadened with delighted amusement. "I can't say it's an interest I share but maybe that might work out for the best, then."

It sounded very much like Gavin intended to make a habit of this. Derrick couldn't decide if the notion alleviated his confusion or not. He didn't have much time to think on it, however, before Gavin took another step forward and brushed his lips across Derrick's. The kiss was soft, inquiring. Gavin's scent surrounded him and Derrick slid his hands up Gavin's arms and around his neck.

"Time for my goofy confession." Derrick felt Gavin's lips curve against his mouth. "I think you taste *wonderful*."

"I don't find that goofy," Derrick murmured with a quiet laugh. His fingers brushed the stubble just below the hairline at the back of Gavin's neck. "Thank you. I'm really, *really* enjoying myself."

Gavin's hands came up, resting on Derrick's chest. He didn't grope, but the pressure of his hands, the heat of his palms over Derrick's nipples made the taut-wire tension that had been pulling on Derrick all day even tighter.

Gavin kissed him again, with no more intent or aggression than before. "I am, too. It just feels good. Very good."

"It does." Derrick deepened the kiss himself, his lips parting, tugging at Gavin's, breaking off to murmur, "I've wanted your hands on me since I walked in the door."

"So have I. It's been really difficult. More so than I ever remember it being. It's a little scary, isn't it? Wanting something this badly."

"Yeah." His skin prickled at how eerily Gavin echoed his own musings. He was getting carried away and he knew it, and everything in him that was cautious and rational kept telling him to pull it back in. But the feeling of being in motion again after so many years was just too heady and wonderful. "I'm not used to it."

"I'm not used to it either. Not like this." Before Derrick could ask Gavin what he meant, Gavin's kisses changed. No longer inquiring, they coaxed, urging Derrick's mouth open. His tongue flicked at Derrick's lips. Slow. Maddeningly gentle.

Derrick heard a low, urgent sound and realized it had come from him. In an instant, Gavin's kiss became harder, firmer, his body pressing against Derrick's. Derrick's hands tightened on Gavin's shoulders, and he moaned into the kiss.

He swallowed once Gavin drew away, his jeans too tight and his pulse too fast. "We gonna stand here in the kitchen all night, then? Not that I mind making out, but sooner or later, not standing up might be a better idea."

"And where would you rather be?"

Tired of skirting around it, he pulled away, meeting Gavin's eyes, frank and determined. "I think you already know. I'm not sure why I'm playing coy. Not sure why either of us are."

Something sad and uncertain passed through Gavin's eyes, his voice dropping as he ducked his head a bit. "Because I want every part of this to be *your* decision. That's why."

Derrick blinked. "I'm not sure what you mean by that. Since I walked through that door the other night, have I given you any reason to believe I'm not into this?"

"No, you haven't." Gavin sighed. "I just don't want to feel like I'm pressuring you. Really, this is all me, not you."

Derrick frowned, trying to reconcile this worry of Gavin's with the self-assured man who'd started out coming on to him so strong.

Was it just the HIV thing? Or a lingering fear of being wrong at every turn, the way he'd said it had been with his ex?

Or was he afraid of *becoming* his ex? Did he really think himself capable of forcing his will on someone else?

Derrick didn't know, and he didn't think now was the best time to ask. Maybe there was a ceiling on how much he should expect Gavin to bare his soul, considering he wasn't exactly coming clean with Gavin himself.

"You're not pressuring me," he answered instead. "Not even a little. If I freeze up from time to time, it's because I have no idea what I'm doing. Not just—not just the sex. Being with someone. Frankly, the guidance helps."

"I'm also afraid of pushing this too fast."

"We might just both be guilty of that," Derrick murmured. "And you know what? I can't seem to find it in me to care."

"Okay. Good." Gavin kissed him hard, aggressively, full of the same brand of *wanting* that had been snarling within Derrick's head all day, itching to break its leash. Which it did, and Derrick clutched at Gavin, groped. They tugged at each other's shirts, ravenous for the touch of flesh.

They ended up on the kitchen floor. Gavin settled between his thighs, his lean back bare under Derrick's grasping fingers. He met the roll of Derrick's hips, the pressure *just right*, and Derrick groaned.

"You feel good." He raked his blunted fingers down Gavin's back, enjoying the way Gavin's spine arched in response. He kissed and nipped and sucked at Gavin's neck and shoulders. Gavin's groans were feral and desperate, his fingers wrenching a moan from Derrick as they pinched his nipples.

God, he was right. It is better when it hurts.

Derrick's arching response brought their cocks rubbing together again, and his fingers dug in to the flesh of Gavin's back. Gavin raised himself up far enough to grasp Derrick's belt and pulled it out of its buckle with an impatient jerk, tugging at the button and zip of his fly. He thrust his hand down Derrick's briefs, gripping his dick, and Derrick's hips came up off the floor.

"*Fuck!*" he groaned, his eyes rolling back in his head for a moment before he opened them again, staring at Gavin wildly. "Oh, God, *please.*"

Gavin continued those firm, limited strokes. "Please, *what?*" he asked, looking almost predatory, his grin tight and savage as he looked down at Derrick.

"*Shit,*" Derrick panted. "I don't know. Anything. Everything. Just… keep going…"

"I will." Gavin's hand kept moving, and Derrick bucked into his grasp, groaning with impatience and pushing at his jeans, trying to work them down over his hips without disrupting Gavin's strokes. He began to laugh as he wriggled and shifted, tickled by the absurdity, and Gavin joined in. The laughter made it even better, for a moment, transforming raw, urgent, frankly scary need into something that was also fun. But then the laughter faded, and the need screamed within them again.

There was nothing amused in Gavin's eyes as he rose, towering over Derrick as he lay on the floor, and opened his own jeans, making a show of each button undone. He pushed them down and kicked them aside, then turned to the counter to look for something. Derrick was pretty sure Gavin deliberately stood so he had a nearly straight-line view up between his legs. The swinging weight of his balls, the crack of his ass, the pale, sparse hair covering the backs of his thighs, tapering off to almost bare skin at the top.

His cock, bobbing before him, driving Derrick wild with the longing to touch and smell and taste.

When Gavin knelt again between Derrick's thighs, he had a small bottle of salad oil in his hand. Derrick licked his lips, no longer thinking of humor, as Gavin drizzled it over his dick, a fair amount of it pooling in the hollow cut-outs before his hips, sliding down the crease of his groin. With what would be his last rational thought for a while, Derrick realized one of them would have to mop the floor in the morning. Then Gavin capped the oil and reached up to set it on the island. He leaned down, bracing a hand on the floor beside Derrick's shoulder and wrapped the other around Derrick's cock.

Derrick groaned, his head rolling back and his eyes snapping shut as Gavin's slick hand began to pump. "Oh! Yeah...."

"No. Look at me." A note of command gave an edge to Gavin's voice, determined and undeniable. The pressure in Derrick's balls tightened; his stomach dropped a bit with something that felt just the closest bit like fear mingling with arousal. When he blinked his eyes open again, Gavin had pulled his lip between his teeth, his eyes hot and intent. His hand curled around the head of Derrick's cock and Derrick struggled to keep his eyes from closing again.

"You look so fucking gorgeous when I do this."

He felt his face heating up, but he couldn't catch his breath enough to demur. His spine arched off the floor, the motion moving like a wave through his body.

Gavin's grip tightened on his cock. "You look gorgeous when you blush, too. Keep moving. Just like that. God, you're so beautiful."

Everything was an exquisite agony of self-consciousness combined with pleasure so intense it almost hurt. His skin was flushed, sweating. His chest heaved as he gasped for each sobbing breath. The only thing more excruciating than the rapid approach of his climax was when Gavin drew his hand away. He swiped it through the oil pooled on Derrick's belly and slicked it over his own cock before he let his knees slide out from under him, his hips pressing flush against Derrick's and their cocks lining up.

Gavin took them both in his long, lean fingers and started pumping, still propped up on one arm.

"Oh, God...." Derrick groaned, lifting his head to peer down the gap between their chests, where the heads of their dicks appeared through the ring of Gavin's lean, elegant fingers, then retreated. Gavin's hips moved, adding to the push.

In the reflection of the glass door of the stove, it looked for all the world like Gavin was fucking him.

Derrick stared at the image, the tension in his balls ratcheting up, screaming and straining toward orgasm. Only Gavin's voice, firm and insistent, drew him away from it.

"Look at me!"

Derrick's eyes gravitated to Gavin's face. It was set, intent, his eyes burning as he stared down at Derrick. His pale skin began to shine with sweat, flushed beneath his freckles. The longer Derrick fought to keep his eyes open, his fingers scrabbling against the cool tile of the floor, the more intense his impending orgasm became. It hovered out of reach, held at bay by the effort of maintaining eye contact.

And finally it burst free, ripping a shout from Derrick's throat. His eyes slammed shut and his face contorted, the pleasure so fucking intense it hurt. The hot spray of his own cum splashed against his skin, and through the pounding of his pulse in his ears and the ragged sound of his own gasping breath, he heard Gavin's soft growl.

"So gorgeous. So *fucking* gorgeous."

The pressure left his cock just as it became too sensitive to continue. His eyes opened, and he stared at Gavin in a daze as Gavin rose up, sitting back on his haunches, his slick hand beginning to move up and down his own cock. He kept his eyes on Derrick's face, and Derrick realized it was a performance.

He watched, rapt. The fingers of Gavin's other hand gathered a small bit of oil not mingled with Derrick's cooling semen, and he reached behind himself.

Derrick echoed Gavin's groan, and Gavin's eyes fluttered as his hand moved.

Gavin's hips rolled in a continuous motion, pushing into his fist before retreating to fuck himself on his finger, then repeating

156

the circuit. Derrick couldn't have torn his eyes away if he wanted to—and he damned sure didn't. Faster, Gavin moved, and faster, the pumping of his fist getting harder, hitting the skin of his groin on each downward thrust with a wet smack. His groans grew louder, his face more strained, agonized.

"Go, Gav," Derrick heard himself murmuring. "I wanna see you come."

"Fuck," Gavin panted, hunching over a little, no longer concerned with putting on a display. His eyes closed, and he focused on jerking himself with fast, firm strokes. His groans became continuous, punctuated by muttered profanities.

Derrick realized what Gavin had meant when he'd called Derrick gorgeous in the moment before his climax. He waited with bated breath, staring as if afraid of missing a single second.

"… *fuck*. Derrick…." Gavin's moan choked off as he went still, shuddering, sliding through his fist as warm streams crossed the cooling mess on Derrick's belly.

Derrick stared at the mingled splashes, fascinated by them as he'd never been by his own. He wanted to touch it, feel it. Swirl it and play with it. Learn it. But Gavin caught his hand as it twitched toward his abdomen.

"You work with your hands," he murmured, almost managing not to sound remorseful. "There could be cuts…."

"Right." Derrick mustered a half-hearted smile as Gavin reached into a nearby drawer and grabbed a dishtowel to clean him off. The cloth was dry, but it would do for the initial cleanup, though he'd need a shower to get the oil off his skin. He felt content and quiet as Gavin tended to him and carefully wadded up the towel. Then he sank down beside Derrick, taking his weight off his knees, and reached out, sliding a hand along Derrick's jaw and drawing him in for a kiss. Derrick sank into it, lassitude setting in, along with a craving to be close to Gavin.

He nuzzled Gavin's neck, breathing in the scent of him, the amazing amalgamation of woodsy cologne and cigarettes and something that was simply *Gavin*. He couldn't be bothered to care what he might be giving away, with the sudden need for closeness, for intimacy. He just had to feel Gavin's arms around him, to feel Gavin's lips against his.

"You're right," he murmured against Gavin's jaw. "That was gorgeous."

Gavin chuckled. "Glad you think so. Ready to get off this floor?"

Nothing sounded better than curling against Gavin in bed, since the ravenous *need* was quiet again. "Think your legs are working yet?"

Another soft chuckle. "I think I can manage. Can you?"

"It might be a near thing, but it's worth the effort."

They gathered up their scattered clothing, making it to the bedroom without incident. Derrick hung his clothes neatly over the back of the chair again and brushed his teeth as Gavin had his last cigarette, then slid into the fresh sheets they'd changed the morning before.

When Gavin climbed into bed, Derrick moved into his arms without delay, refusing to let himself analyze this unprecedented neediness. He lay his head on Gavin's shoulder, draping his arm across Gavin's stomach and hooking his knee over Gavin's thighs.

"I like this," Gavin whispered, his lips against Derrick's forehead as his gentle fingers combed through Derrick's hair.

I do, too. Maybe too much for my own good.

He wouldn't let himself say it.

"So do I," he murmured, closing his eyes with a sigh.

CHAPTER FOURTEEN

MORNING SEX, Derrick thought deliriously, panting in the aftermath, was definitely something he could get used to.

Gavin released his too-sensitive cock, wiping him with a sheet, while Gavin's own dick still softened against the cleft of Derrick's ass. His semen cooled between Gavin's belly and Derrick's back as the rocking of his hips, the pantomime of fucking he'd chased to its climax against Derrick's back, ceased.

Derrick turned his face toward the pillow, gasping ragged breaths. He could still hear Gavin's voice, low and growly in his ear, making vulgar demands.

You sound so sexy when you beg.

Derrick finally found his voice. "How do you manage that?"

"Manage what?"

"Being so insanely sexy?" he asked with a breathless, giddy laugh, not entirely sure he could think clearly enough to speak sense.

Gavin chuckled behind his ear. "I'm flattered."

Derrick smiled, still feeling dazed, high. "It's true. That was about the hottest thing ever."

"Oh, I dunno. Give me time." He could hear the grin in Gavin's voice, low with sexy promise. "I guess that was more than the couple of minutes we'd planned."

Derrick chuckled, the sound transforming to a full-throated laugh. "Yeah, I guess so. Sorry."

"Why would you be sorry for that?" Gavin panted, his voice amused.

Derrick laughed harder. Could it be possible to actually be high from sex?

"I lied. I'm not. Not even a little. Damn, I'm having fun."

Gavin echoed the laugh, and Derrick felt him kiss the back of his neck. He closed his eyes, the gesture replacing humor with a surge of tenderness.

"So am I," Gavin agreed in a murmur. "I wish we didn't have to get out of bed at all, but...."

Derrick sighed, nodded. "Yeah. I don't get sick days, and today my client's a real piece of work. I shouldn't be late. Guess we should get to the shower, huh?"

He felt Gavin's nod. "Yeah, we should. Separate, so we don't get distracted again."

"Oh. Right. Yeah. Probably a good idea, there."

Gavin chuckled. "Go ahead, then. I'll start the coffee while you shower."

Pulling away from Gavin's body was far harder than he could ever have imagined it being. He made himself do it, wanting nothing more than to find a reason to stay for another minute, or another hour.

Instead, he turned and gave Gavin a soft kiss. "Good morning."

"Good morning." Gavin slid a hand along his jaw and into his hair, kissing him in return.

Breaking off, Derrick drew away, doing his best to wipe his back with the sheet he knew they'd be changing anyway before picking up his overnight bag and padding to the bathroom off the bedroom closet.

The bedroom smelled faintly of cigarette smoke from Gavin passing through when he emerged from the shower. In the other bathroom, he could hear the shower running. He couldn't smell coffee wafting through the apartment, but he figured it was due to the French press Gavin used instead of a drip-brewer. Laying his clean clothes over the chair, he located the linen closet and grabbed a fresh set of sheets, stripping the bed and dropping the stained linens into the washer before returning to spread the fresh ones. He'd start the washing machine once Gavin had finished with his shower.

As he replaced the bedspread, laying it out with his back to the bedroom door, he heard Gavin behind him.

"Wow. Now this is a great sight."

Derrick straightened from where he bent over the bed, a hot flush creeping up from his chest.

Maybe leaving his jeans and shirt off to avoid staining them with any of the fresh semen on the sheets hadn't been such a great idea.

Gavin's hand ghosted over his ass, and Gavin's lips pressed against the back of his shoulder.

"You're blushing now, aren't you?"

Derrick laughed, self-conscious. "That's not fair."

"Hm, maybe not, but it's fun. And sexy." Gavin stepped back. "Thank you for changing the sheets. You didn't have to do that."

Derrick shrugged. "Why not? Needed to be done, and I had a few minutes to spare." He gave the bedspread one last twitch, tucking it around the pillows, then crossed to the chair to grab his jeans.

"Well, thank you," Gavin murmured. "There's coffee in the kitchen for you."

Gavin disappeared into the master bath again, where Derrick imagined he kept most of his toiletries. He still felt damp after his shower, even in the air-conditioned apartment, hinting that it would be a humid day outside. He opted to leave his shirt off, the top button of his jeans undone to keep it from rubbing against his belly, and headed out to the kitchen.

On the counter sat a cup of coffee lightened with cream. Derrick thought it was Gavin's until he noticed the note the cup rested upon.

Enjoy your coffee.

He smiled at the note. He hadn't had a chance to try Gavin's coffee yet. They'd had coffee at Derrick's house Saturday morning, of which Gavin had taken one dutiful sip before he set the cup aside and ignored it, leaving Derrick with the impression he didn't care for it.

Derrick didn't usually take cream or sugar, but he took a sip and hummed in approval. Gavin hadn't over-sweetened it, and the coffee was rich and mellow.

"Like it, then?" Gavin asked, coming down the hall with a suit jacket in his hands, which he folded over the back of one of the barstools.

Derrick forgot about the coffee, staring. Every time he'd seen Gavin on a weekday, it had been after work, when he was a little rumpled, no longer clean-shaven, his tie missing and his collar unbuttoned.

He looked different in the morning. Sharper. More gorgeous. His hair, which he wore so tousled on the weekend, had been neatly combed back. His shirt was crisply ironed and his tie impeccably knotted. Derrick was willing to bet his suit pants had been custom-tailored to fit him so well.

He had to quell the sudden urge to undo all that neat grooming and leave Gavin rumpled again, and nodded, remembering the coffee. "It's good. Really good."

Gavin grinned, preparing a cup for himself from the French press on the breakfast bar. "I think it's worth the effort. Makes my Mondays better, at least."

He knows he looks good.

Gavin knew, and he was proud of it, Derrick realized. The light chatter about the coffee was just a cover. He wanted Derrick to see him looking gorgeous. Derrick knew he should say something, compliment Gavin, but anything that came to mind sounded trite or clumsy.

Gavin trailed a finger down Derrick's bare chest, and Derrick felt his nipples tighten.

"I like the view, here." He stepped closer, kissing Derrick's collarbone. "If *every* Monday could begin like this...."

Derrick set his coffee aside, his arms encircling Gavin's torso. He took a breath, keeping his tone neutral. "I don't think I'd mind that a bit. Maybe we should make a habit of this."

Gavin grinned again. "Maybe we should. Though with the busy day I'm sure you've got ahead of you, we should probably get a better breakfast in you than coffee and an orgasm, hm?"

"Guess we should." He kissed Gavin, keeping it soft, but unable to resist the urge to have his hands on Gavin just a moment longer. God knew he'd be doing a hell of a lot more if time weren't an issue.

He forced himself to turn away and locate the paper bag of bagels he'd brought with him to tide him over until he could get a full breakfast on the way to his morning job. He sliced two and put them on a tray in the toaster oven. As they cooked, he opened the refrigerator to rummage for the cream cheese and stopped cold.

"You bought breakfast foods."

"Yeah," Gavin said softly. "I did."

Such a little thing. Why was he at a loss again?

He could demur, protest that Gavin didn't have to do that sort of thing for him. He could freeze up, over-think it all, trying to figure out just what it meant that Gavin wanted him over regularly enough to do such a thing. He could let himself get scared again, terrified at the idea of becoming too attached, too dependent.

Nothing lasted. He knew that. People left, sooner or later. They died or they walked away and went on with their lives while he was alone and hurting. The best he could manage would be to try to minimize the damage.

He could pull back, guard himself against the day that happened. Hide away like he had for the last decade.

Or he could accept it, and keep moving forward, taking things as they came.

"Thank you," he murmured, pulling out some berries and cottage cheese to go along with the bagels.

"You're welcome."

Swallowing hard, he pushed aside the fear. "You'll call me later? I really should stay at my house tonight. Chelsea's been alone too much. But other than that, I don't have any plans."

"Of course I'll call," Gavin assured him.

"I check my cell phone pretty regularly, since it's my main business line. I'm hoping I'll be done with this job by mid-afternoon. If you wanted to see each other tonight, you're welcome to come over."

Gavin smiled over his coffee mug. "Should I bring dinner? Or perhaps pick up some beer on my way?"

"Beer sounds good. I'll cook. Yesterday I set a rib roast to marinate overnight." He ducked his head. "I was hoping you'd say yes."

Gavin grinned. "And should I stop by here and pick up another suit before I go?"

"If you're okay getting ready for work someplace else, I'd really like that."

"All right. I'll call you when I leave work, then."

"That sounds perfect." Derrick pushed his empty plate aside, wiping his mouth before sliding off his stool to kiss Gavin. "Thank you."

Gavin returned the kiss, taking his time. His hand cupped Derrick's cheek, stroking with soft fingers. "I'll probably call you around five or five-thirty."

Derrick opened his eyes, a bit glassy, once again wanting nothing more to drag Gavin back to bed. Not even for sex, necessarily. As with last night on the kitchen floor, something that had happened this morning made him feel like he *needed* to be close Gavin.

With effort, he answered. "I'll be sure to keep my phone on me. If it goes to voice mail, I'm probably in the middle of a job and can't let myself get distracted. I'll check it as soon as I can, though." He chuckled. "Now I just have to make sure I'm home in time to clean up the stack of dirty videos piled up by the TV in my bedroom."

Gavin laughed in delight. "See, that's why porn on the computer is so much easier. All I had to do was make sure you didn't open my laptop."

"I'm too paranoid about viruses, I guess." Still chuckling, Derrick began to clean up the breakfast dishes.

Gavin sat at the bar, continuing to sip his coffee. "You just have to be careful. Anyway, clean them up if you'd really like. I wouldn't mind either way. I hear you can tell a lot about a man by his porn. Or maybe I'm just making that up."

Derrick glanced over his shoulder, meeting Gavin's grin with one of his own. "Huh. Then maybe I should have a look at your laptop after all."

"Next time. We'll both be late for work if I pulled it out right now and you know it."

"Yeah, I do," he said a touch wistfully, washing the dishes by hand and propping them in the drying rack. "Or you could just tell me what I'd find on there. Sometime."

"Sometime, I might just do that." Gavin slipped off his bar stool and came up behind Derrick, putting an arm around him. "God, I wish I didn't have to go to work today."

It helped, a little, knowing his reluctance to be apart, this need to be near Gavin, was shared. Derrick had no idea why but he felt downright clingy, trying his best to keep it in check.

"I do, too," he answered, drying off his hands and turning to Gavin. "Those buttons on your shirt are just begging to be opened one by one."

"I notice you didn't mention the tie."

Derrick slid his hands down to ride at Gavin's waist. "I *would* have to get rid of that to get to the buttons, now, would I?" he hummed, pondering. "Tug it slowly loose from your collar, that sort of thing?"

"Yeah, that sort of thing." Gavin closed his eyes, his lips curving.

Derrick's hand came up, stroking the side of Gavin's neck. "I really should go finish getting dressed."

Nodding, Gavin released him, and Derrick made himself walk away.

When he emerged from the bedroom with his overnight bag slung over his shoulder, Gavin had his laptop case packed and his suit jacket on. Derrick started the washing machine on his way back down the hall to the living room.

"When you come over tonight, you might wanna bring your little coffee maker."

Gavin laughed at the description of his French press. "Okay, I'll do that. I'll even bring my beans." Derrick watched as Gavin did a conscientious inventory, making sure he had everything he needed.

Outside the entrance of Gavin's apartment building, they paused.

"My truck's parked down there," Derrick murmured, pointing in the opposite direction of Gavin's car. "How okay are you with your neighbors seeing us saying good-bye?"

Gavin shrugged, smiling. "I don't have anything to hide. Unless you intend to shove your hand down my pants. Then I might have an issue with it."

"Don't tempt me," Derrick murmured. He grabbed Gavin lightly by the tie and tugged him forward, kissing him briefly and firmly, then straightened Gavin's glasses for him. "Okay then. Have a good day."

Gavin gave him a delighted grin, adjusting the damage done to his careful Windsor knot. "You, too. I'll call you later."

Smiling, somehow feeling lighter about the prospect of the day apart and the evening to come, Derrick turned and made his way to his truck.

AN EXCERPT FROM

ACCELERATION

IMPULSE, BOOK TWO

GAINING MOMENTUM

GAVIN HAYES IS EVERYTHING DERRICK COULD ASK FOR IN A LOVER. Gorgeous. Passionate. Great in bed. Derrick finds it very easy to just let himself go, to let Gavin guide him and teach him all the things he missed during a decade of celibacy. In the course of a single weekend, Derrick's routine is transformed, his mornings and evenings filled with sex. Sweet, seductive, wild or raunchy, Gavin offers to him all the pleasure he's denied himself for so long.

But learning how to be a lover in bed is one thing. Learning to be one out of bed is another. For Derrick, being alone has become habit. Sharing his confidences doesn't come nearly as readily as sharing his bed. And after so many losses, the last thing Derrick wants is to become dependent upon another person who might not always be there.

And Gavin always being there is far from certain. With an ex-lover lurking in the background, and the question of Gavin's future health still outstanding, neither Gavin nor Derrick feel capable of asking for anything more than right now. But neither will Gavin be kept on the fringes of Derrick's life. Can Derrick let someone in, before the opportunity passes him by?

AS HE SAT AT THE TABLE, Derrick could still feel the kiss Gavin had given him when he walked in the door. Nothing more than a simple peck of greeting. It had been easy. Effortless. Natural. He wasn't sure what to make of the fact that, on their third night together, he and Gavin were developing the sort of comfortable and casual intimacies that came with deeper relationships than this undefined *whatever* they had.

Friday night had been an impulse. Derrick had been filled with wild need when he'd shown up on Gavin's doorstep. Sunday had been more deliberate, planning to stay over at Gavin's.

Now it was Monday.

Maybe we should make a habit of this, he'd suggested earlier, before they'd left for work. Gavin had taken him up on the offer.

Habit. Habit was a good word for it.

Could three nights be deemed a habit?

Gavin sniffed, closing his eyes as he seated himself. "Ah. Smells like Friday."

"Huh?" Derrick gave him a quizzical look.

"Shabbat. The Sabbath. Mom used to always make roast beef for dinner before we went to services."

Derrick laughed softly. "Oh, right. Sorry. You'd think I'd have put that together, the number of times my friends have had me over to dinner on Friday before Devon and I go to play pool while his wife goes to services."

Gavin shrugged, taking a drink of his beer. "I was a little vague."

"I'll keep that in mind for Fridays from here on out, though." Derrick bit his tongue as he realized what he'd said.

Habit. Right.

Derrick ducked his head and cut his roast to keep his hands busy. Luckily Gavin let the remark slide.

Or maybe not.

"I hope so. You know it's a good deed, practically a commandment, to have sex on Shabbat?"

Derrick felt his face flush. Was Gavin *trying* to fluster him? "Does that, um… apply to gay guys, too?"

"It should." Gavin gave him a smug smile, which made Derrick fumble his knife. He tilted his head, regarding Derrick with a slight wrinkle forming between his brows. "Are you nervous about something?"

Derrick frowned, puzzled at his own raw-edged nerves. He'd been feeling short of breath and antsy since before Gavin arrived, and he couldn't explain it any more than he could explain why the kiss hello had surprised him.

"I guess I am."

"Why?"

"I have no idea," he said, glancing across the table at Gavin. "I've been looking forward to this all day."

Gavin smiled. "Good. So have I."

"I-I mean, I guess it's different, somehow. Here. This house."

"Oh? How so?"

Derrick shook his head, shrugging helplessly. "I'm not sure. Maybe because I've never done it before? Had anyone over here, I mean. Well, I-I've had company, of course, people have come to visit. Guests. Friends. That sort of thing." He begun babbling, which was a minor miracle in itself, but he didn't seem to be capable of shutting up and, *dear God*, why couldn't he shut up? "But not like this."

"You mean you've never slept with someone here."

And now he was blushing again. Great. Just great.

Gavin grinned, delighted by the blush. Of course.

"Yeah. Exactly." He and LeeAnn had made out up in his room all the time in high school, naturally, but by the time they'd begun having sex during her vacations from college, he'd been too immersed in taking care of his grandparents to ever consider having her over to the house for any length of time. Sex had been something they'd managed in the short, hurried interludes when

Miss Ingrid had shooed him out the door and taken over for a couple hours here and there.

"And why does it feel different than over at my place?"

"I don't know." Derrick shook his head again. He suspected he did know, but it wasn't something he could say. Having Gavin overnight here in his home made everything more real. This thing with Gavin wasn't something which happened elsewhere, outside and apart from his normal existence. He wasn't just bringing Gavin into his bed. He was bringing Gavin into his *life*.

And over-thinking in the process.

"Are you still okay with this?"

Derrick nodded, meeting Gavin's gaze as he reached for his beer. "Yeah. I am. It's just all new. But I meant what I said. I've looked forward to this all day. Just… now I feel like I can't catch my breath, and all I can think about is last night and this morning."

"In a good way?" Gavin asked, an edge of caution in his tone as he took a drink of his own beer.

Derrick nodded, cutting into his roast. "It was incredible."

"What part?" Gavin gave him an assessing look. He ate calmly, as though whatever had such a profound effect on Derrick barely registered with him.

"I don't know. They way you… the way you talked to me, maybe?"

Gavin, kneeling over him on the kitchen floor. Gavin's hand jerking him off. Gavin's cock rocking against the cleft of his ass.

Gavin's voice, commanding him.

Look at me! No. Don't hide your face. Let me hear that voice of yours. You sound so sexy when you beg.

"You liked that?"

Derrick nodded, trying to eat slowly, to downplay just how horny the memory made him.

"Good." Gavin said, satisfied. He leaned back in his chair once he finished interrogating Derrick. "I won't lie; I do enjoy doing that."

Enjoy doing what, exactly? Derrick wondered. What had Gavin done to make the last twenty-four hours so amazing? He hadn't said much, or even talked all that dirty. But what he *had* said, those simple commands, had driven Derrick wild.

"I, um, don't think I'll have a problem with that." He wasn't sure exactly what he'd agreed to, but whatever it was, he wanted more of it.

"I'll keep that in mind." They fell silent as they continued eating. When Chelsea finished her own food, she approached the archway from the kitchen to the dining room. The overhead light from the kitchen shone on her bristly fawn-sable coat. Gavin shook his head with an amused smile.

"I can't get over it. She has enough loose skin to make another dog."

"She's a shar pei. Comes with the breed," Derrick chuckled, glad for a distraction from the pounding of his blood in his ears and the struggle not to squirm against the tightness of his jeans. He gave Chelsea a look as she stepped over the line where the linoleum met the carpet.

"Uh-uh," he said firmly, pointing the the kitchen floor. "You know better."

Chelsea hung her wrinkled head repentantly and lay down on her belly with her paws just touching the threshold.

Gavin glanced over at her and smiled. "You've got her well-trained."

Derrick quirked up one corner of his mouth in a half-smile, and murmured, "Keep an eye on her, but don't make it obvious you're watching. She likes to test me."

They continued eating in silence. After a moment, Chelsea inched forward, creeping on her belly, just over the line. She did it again when no one reprimanded her. Soon her paws had crossed the threshold up to the joints, while her muzzle still rested on them, trying to appear as inoffensive as when she'd been laying where she was supposed to be.

Derrick snapped his fingers and her head came up with a start. "Back to your spot."

Obediently, she slid back, her brown eyes woeful, and Gavin chuckled. "She does this every time?"

Derrick shrugged with an affectionate smile. "Not all the time, but usually, especially when I'm cooking something that smells good to her. Or when I'm distracted by company. She likes to test who's top dog, see if she can get away with giving herself a promotion in the pack."

Gavin grinned, and dropped his voice to a lower register. "So, you like being top dog?"

Derrick's mouth went dry and he took a long drink of his beer. Damn. He'd walked into that one. Gavin still managed to catch him out with unexpected bits of innuendo.

"Do you?" It wasn't an answer, but it was better than *How the hell am I supposed to know?*

Gavin's grin spread, became a bit predatory. "I would've thought it was obvious. Though I can be versatile."

Derrick cleared his throat, pushing aside his empty plate. "Good to know."

Gavin's grin persisted, his gaze keen. Did he mean to make Derrick squirm? And if so, why?

As he wrapped up the leftovers and washed the dishes, Derrick wondered how long it would take before he stopped reacting this way. When would every moment he spent in Gavin's company stop being filled with unnerving expectation, every action just passing time until the next touch? When would every word no longer be an opportunity for verbal foreplay?

It felt good. Fun. Wild. Delirious. But terrifying and out of control, also. When would he regain his footing so he could feel like he stood on stable ground once more?

Gavin brought in the last of the dishes from the table, bowls with sponge cake crumbs and remnants of blueberry juice and whipped cream clinging to the sides.

"And what did you plan for us to do after dinner?" he asked with a smile.

Derrick swallowed. Was he the only one who had expected they'd go straight to bed? Had Gavin planned to be entertained? Would Derrick be demanding, or worse, pathetic, to want to jump right to sex?

Was that all he was after, here? Or had the years of abstinence just made him want to glut himself on pleasure all at once?

"I hadn't thought very far ahead. I got to dessert, then my brain just sort of shut down." It was about as close he could come to admitting the only thing he could think of was sex.

Gavin chuckled. "Well, what do you usually do in the evenings?"

"Nothing exciting, I promise," Derrick murmured, his tone touched with self-deprecation. "Hang out with Chelsea. Watch some TV. Play a game, if I'm not working on making something for a client."

"Well, we could start there," Gavin offered. "I don't do much different in the evenings myself, so I don't mind."

He stacked the last of the dishes on the drying rack and drained the sink, wiping it down. Then, with his head bowed over the sink, Derrick closed his eyes and clenched his jaw. He gripped the edge of the counter, his knuckles whitening.

How could Gavin not *feel* this same insatiable need? How was it only him? Was he more into it than Gavin was?

"I don't wanna watch TV with you, Gav." His murmur was calm and low, but honest.

Gavin stepped close, the fabric of his dress shirt and suit pants brushing against Derrick's simple t-shirt and jeans. Slowly, Derrick turned to face him.

"I don't want to watch TV with you, either."

175

He thrust his hands roughly into Derrick's hair and kissed him, hard.

Yes. This. Derrick groaned, all the eager expectation that had been thrumming inside him since they'd parted that morning finally breaking into action. His arms slid around Gavin's chest, caressing the fine cotton of his shirt. His body relaxed against Gavin's with a low, grateful moan.

Each detail became it's own knee-weakening point of focus. Gavin's tongue in his mouth, Gavin's hands clenching in his hair, then moving down to grip his shirt. Derrick's fingers dug into Gavin's back as Gavin reached his waist and tugged his shirt up out of his jeans. Then those long, lean fingers were on his skin, stroking across his stomach.

"God, your hands…." Derrick moaned between kisses.

He let his head fall back, offering Gavin more liberty to move down to his neck, nipping and sucking. Gavin's teeth closed gently over the junction of his shoulder and neck, gradually increasing the pressure. Derrick sagged against the counter as Gavin's thumbs rubbed circles around his nipples.

He panted as the bite on his neck edged closer to pain, drooping with relief and disappointment when Gavin eased off.

"We really… ought to get… to the bedroom," he murmured as Gavin dragged his tongue along the impressions left by his teeth. "Before I can't walk."

Gavin laughed softly and stepped back, looking satisfied with himself. "Go, then. I'll be right behind you."

Derrick nodded once, a brief, jerky movement, before bending to unlace his work boots and kick them off. He jerked his shirt over his head as he went, trying to walk at a normal pace down the hall. He wanted to give himself time, to draw back from the frenetic *need* welling up inside him, pushing him toward desperation.

Without warning, Gavin's hands closed over Derrick's upper arms. He propelled Derrick chest-first against the wall, pressing along Derrick's back. His voice rasped behind Derrick's ear, "I've been wanting to do this all day."

A nudge of his hips against Derrick's ass clarified just what he meant.

"God, yes," Derrick whispered, his eyes closing as he rested his heated cheek against the cool, painted drywall.

Gavin ground against him harder. "Have you been thinking about this, too?" he murmured. "Thinking about what I did this morning when I came against your back? Were you distracted while you were working?"

Hard. Everything was hard, physically and mentally. He was caught between the wall and the pressure of Gavin's erection. His own dick, trapped inside his jeans, found nothing yielding to ease the ache.

His thoughts came only with monumental effort. His pride, his need to control this headlong plummet into... whatever this was... struggled between giving Gavin the admission he sought and trying to retain his dignity.

Truth and need won over reserve. He pushed his ass back against Gavin, seeking more.

"Yes. God. All damn day... couldn't stop thinking about you...."

Gavin's fingers slid down his ribs, ghosting along the sensitive line of skin above the waistband of his jeans. "Tell me, what did you think about? Did you imagine more? Build upon what I did, make it into a fantasy? When you got home after your morning job, did you jerk off after you had lunch?" Gavin's voice dropped lower, barely a whisper as his lips brushed the shell of Derrick's ear. His hot breath blowing strands of Derrick's hair against his cheek. "Did you call my name when you came?"

The sound Derrick made was humiliatingly close to a whimper as he moved, restless, urgent need driving him.

"I did." The admission came in a thoughtless torrent, spilling from his mouth without any deliberation. "All day, it was all I could see. Couldn't wait to get home. Every delay just drove me a little more crazy...."

Gavin rocked against Derrick's ass again. His fingers quickly unbuckled Derrick's belt and slipped into the snug gap between his jeans and his waist.

"What else did you think about, then?" he asked, nipping at Derrick's earlobe. One hand drew out of Derrick's waistband to cup over the bulge under his fly; the other slid up to pinch his nipple. "Tell me. I want to know just what dirty fantasies you spin up in that gorgeous head of yours."

"Oh, God, please...." Derrick moaned, feeling mindless, delirious with wanting.

"Tell me."

His throat locked against the words he wanted to say. He fought against the verbal paralysis and tried to find a way to admit that he'd stopped by the adult bookstore where he bought his porn today to make a different sort of purchase. Not just condoms, but a better brand of lube than the stuff he grabbed at the pharmacy for jerking off. He'd done it knowing this moment, this decision, might come, possibly tonight.

Trapped between Gavin and the wall, his clothes hanging half-off and Gavin grinding against his ass, why was it the prospect of *words* that made him feel exposed and vulnerable?

What if Gavin didn't want it, or was too afraid? What if the pantomimes of fucking they'd done were as far as Gavin was willing—or comfortable enough—to go? He didn't *think* Gavin would be repulsed, not after the way he'd rimmed Derrick to within an inch of his sanity the other morning. But was it even a good idea? Was it just too damned soon?

How could he be willing to trust Gavin with the act, without being willing to trust Gavin with the confession that he wanted it in the first place?

"I... oh, God...." Gavin's hands tightened, both on his nipple and around the ridge of his cock beneath his fly. The words, when

Derrick forced them from his throat, came out much more coy than he would have liked. "I wondered what it'd be like… if you'd… gone further…."

"Further? You're wondering what it would've been like if I'd fucked you this morning?" Gavin's voice was smooth, steady, controlled. And yet it *seemed* to growl.

Derrick nodded, his cheek sliding against the wall.

"I admit, I've thought about it. Imagined the noises you'd make. How you'd move."

Derrick moaned as Gavin's had slid up and down his bulge with deliberate intent. "Yeah… Oh, God, yeah…."

Gavin dropped his hand from Derrick's chest down to his fly and opened it quickly, pushing his jeans down his hips before pressing him to the cool wall again. The pressure of Gavin's erection against his ass was all the more keen without the extra layer of denim between them.

"Is this what you want?" Gavin murmured in the same low, insistent tone. "You want me to fuck you until you can't see straight?"

Derrick swallowed hard, nodding again, trying to pull himself back enough to make it clear he wasn't just carried away.

"Yeah," he said soberly. "Yeah, I want it."

"You have what we need?" Gavin's voice took on a serious note as well. "I won't do it, otherwise."

Derrick blinked at the question, surprised for a moment that Gavin wouldn't have brought his own supply of condoms and lube. He wondered if Gavin was testing him, seeing if this was something Derrick had truly thought through.

"Yeah. There's a bag. In the bedside table." He glanced over his shoulder, seeking both to reassure Gavin, and seeking reassurance.

Gavin smiled, kissing Derrick. He started at Derrick's mouth, gently, and moved down to his neck, his teeth scraping. His fingers brushed teasingly over the length of Derrick's cock, straining against the navy cotton of his briefs.

"Out of the pants," Gavin murmured. His tone was soft, but it wasn't a request. "Into the bedroom. Now."

Derrick obeyed.

About the Author

AMELIA C. GORMLEY MAY SEEM LIKE ANYONE ELSE. But the truth is she sings in the shower, dances doing laundry, and writes blisteringly hot m/m erotic romance while her five year old is in school. When she's not writing in her Pacific Northwest home, Amelia single-handedly juggles her husband, her son, their home, and the obstacles of life by turning into a everyday superhero. And that, she supposes, is just like anyone else. Her second and third novellas from the *Impulse* Trilogy are also available through this and other fine booksellers.

You can find Amelia in the following places:

www.AMELIACGORMLEY.com

GOODREADS.com
TWITTER.com (@ACGORMLEY)
FACEBOOK.com

Made in the USA
San Bernardino, CA
16 August 2013